CHAUNCEY

1/2/2015

By Gary D Logan

This book is a work of historical fiction. Although some of the characters and events were real, the majority of incidents that occur and the interactions with secondary characters are totally fictional. Any relation to real events is part of the writer's imagination and actions that transpire are imaginary

If you are related to, or have knowledge of the Jacob Miller, Stutzman or Logan families from the Goshen, Indiana area, I would be excited to hear from you.

Thank you again to my wife Marsha who has shown much patience with me while I was writing and researching this story, and for her suggestions in developing the story line. Her courage and positive attitude in the face of persistent health problems has been a tremendous example to me for being persistent in my writing.

Thank you also to my son-in-law Joshua Martin, for his expertise in editing the book and helping with the cover design.

I hope you take pleasure in reading this story as much as I enjoyed writing it.

Available from Amazon.com, CreateSpace.com, and other retail outlets

Contents   Page

Chapter 1   Bart

The mind of little Bart Decker was warped from the normal at a very early age. There was violence in his home during all hours of the day. Nights should have been peaceful, but that too was filled with hostilities when Bart's father would come home from his drinking binges which sometimes lasted for days. The yelling and screaming often would wake up young Bart all hours of the night. The beatings and whippings caused young Bart to retreat into his own secluded world. The word "love" and "kindness" not only were never used, they were never demonstrated. He was taught to fight by his brother that was only two years older. He learned to kill when he was six years old. The father went hunting and Bart followed behind him to see what his pa was doing. Not that his father wanted him to come along; he just followed his Pa because he was bored. The father knew he was being followed, but ignored his small boy as he usually did.

The father came upon a clearing in the forest that had numerous animal prints leading to a small stream running through the center. He squatted behind a large oak tree that bordered the woods. Young Bart inadvertently stepped on a large twig and it made a loud crack in the forest silence. Father jumped up and grabbed Bart harshly by the arm and jerked him over behind the oak where he pushed him to the ground. He hissed in a muffled rage.

"Boy, don't you know how to be quiet? Why did you

follow me anyway? You just spooked any animals within a mile of here. Now sit there and don't make a sound."

Bart rubbed his arm where he had been grabbed. It felt like his shoulder had come apart. But he knew better than to speak or whine. He remembered what happened to his ma when she talked back to him. He saw the bruises that were left on her arms and face. He sat in silence and watched the stream. It seemed so peaceful here, yet his stomach was churning from fear that he might do something else wrong. He felt that discomfort quite often.

Bart sat quietly for what seemed like half a day. He now wished that he had never followed his pa. Just then Bart's dad jabbed him in the shoulder and pointed to a deer approaching the stream from the opposite bank. He put his finger to his lips and mouthed.
        "You shoot him."

Bart's heart raced. He had shot his dad's rifle before several times. It kinda hurt his shoulder, and his shoulder already throbbed. His dad handed the rifle to him and cocked the hammer as he passed it. Then he pointed to the deer and mimicked aiming a rifle and pulling the trigger with his index finger. He hesitated and his pa gestured again impatiently. Bart slowly raised the heavy rifle and winced as a pain shot through his shoulder. His father didn't notice. He was intently watching the deer.

Bart looked down the long barrel and put the front site bead right between the "V" at the rear of the gun. His breathing was coming fast now as he had never shot at anything but tin cans before. He slowly aimed for the chest of the deer above and behind the front legs. He squeezed the trigger. "Blam."

The rifle fired and the woods seemed to mute all of its normal noises. Bart saw the deer lurch forward and then fall. His ears were ringing so loudly they almost hurt. He looked down at his hands. They were shaking. He kind of expected his father to tell him that he had done well or that he was a good shot. When he looked up, his father was already half-way across the stream. He yelled back to Bart.
"Come on boy, ya gotta gut what ya kill."

This was Bart's introduction to killing. The lesson was learned and remembered. The lesson being: fear is a useful tool, even if it is your own fear, but better if it was others fear of him. Bart grew rapidly in his youth and was always tall for his age. He also grew in his meanness and disregard for others---just like his father. Most children learned to steer a wide path around the emerging tyrant. If they didn't, they paid the price.
"Gimme your money. Gimme your lunch. Gimme a kiss." Or there was a punch that meant get out of my way. Whatever Bart wanted, he usually got. His nastiness was not challenged. In Bart's mind this was all justification to further escalate his bullying. It was what people expected of him.

At fifteen years of age he got into a real battle with his father over money taken from his wallet. He was already bigger than his pa and his pa was drunk. Bart beat his father nearly to death. He told his mother he hated her, took the remainder of their money, and then ran away from home. He worked at several menial jobs: cleaning horse stalls, weeding fields, and sweeping floors at a local store but in each job he would get fired for stealing. During this period he befriended a boy that reinforced Bart's bullying ways. His name was

Buster Lee Lukas, nicknamed Bull for short. Bull was an appropriate name for Buster. He was built like one. He was several inches taller than Bart, who by age sixteen was six foot two inches.

Bart was a lanky 185 pounds but Buster was a husky, muscular 265 pounds and proportionally tougher than Bart. Bart always considered himself smarter than Bull. He joked that Bull couldn't manage to tie his own shoes unless he helped him. This was rather irritating to Bull, but he admired his friend---his only true friend. Bull had grown up in a large family. His father had run off when Bull was four years old and left his wife to take care of five kids. Bart knew that as long he had Bull as his friend, there would be few people that would ever challenge him. Together, the two boys were like a ten foot barbed wire fence. You knew that you shouldn't attempt to cross it, but if you tried, you would surely get cut to pieces.

The two boy/men mostly indulged themselves in petty larceny, stealing from innocent persons or from vacant houses. Bart was always the instigator and leader. They soon escalated from petty larceny to vandalizing stores and confronting store owners physically. Most owners in their right mind gave them what they wanted or wished they had. The county authorities in Kentucky where they lived, heard rumors about the duo's wayward conduct, but they could not find even one person that was willing to testify against them. The longer they went without prosecution, the bolder Bart and Buster became. Further escalation occurred when guns became part of their modus operandi and liquor became their trigger. When they got liquored up, they became more violent and bolder than normal. If anything about them was normal.

Chauncey

One Friday afternoon they were drunker than skunks and decided it would be fun to rob a bank. They went into the town of Harlan, Kentucky. They knew that the bank always had a lot of cash on Fridays to pay the coal miners that cashed their paychecks on Friday evenings. They went into the bank waving their pistols and announced:

"We're here to take your money. Everyone put up yer hans and don't make no moves or we'll ssshoot yer ass."

The bank manager thought it was a joke as the two were obviously drunk and stumbling as well as slurring their words badly. He made the mistake of walking toward them and saying.

"Why don't you boys go home and sober up before you get hurt."

Bart shot the man right in the chest. Everyone screamed. Bart climbed over the counter and stuffed as much money in his pockets as he could, and then stumbled out the back door. Bull was shocked that Bart had actually shot a man. He wondered if maybe Bart was out of control.

After running into a wooded area several miles from town, they sat down and counted all of the money. They had stolen a grand total of 1,273 dollars. That made it all worthwhile, thought Bart. After sobering up the two of them decided that the best course of action would be to get out of Kentucky as quickly as possible.

Chapter 2   The Event

T he two of them had been traveling over a week since they had high-tailed it out of Kentucky. The local law was looking for two bank robbers, who suspiciously fit their description.   Bart and Buster's likeness was placed on wanted posters which were widely distributed throughout southern Kentucky. The bank manager was a well liked man in the area. He died of his bullet wound. The people in the bank were the first that were willing to identify the two by name and description.   Buster had been unusually quiet after the bank job. He was not sure if shooting people was part of who he was: however beating them half to death was. He was the "omega" member of the duo. Meaning that, were they a wolf pack, Buster would have his tail between his legs and would roll onto his back in submission to Bart. If Bart were challenged by an outsider though, Buster would without a doubt tear them apart to protect his "alpha" leader.

When the two of them travelled north from Harlan, Kentucky they advanced through Louisville into the state of Indiana. They followed trails and rivers in a general northerly direction. Bart knew that he couldn't leave a trail of crime crumbs so that their travels could be traced. Often they slept in abandoned cabins along their way, or found shelter in caves.   When passing through towns they would separate and go into stores or taverns alone. One would buy extra food or supplies and take it to the other. Never would they be seen together in populated areas nor would they commit any crimes of notoriety. They were running low on cash as they journeyed into the northern part of Indiana. The money from the bank robbery had run out, they were tired of walking, and they needed to eat. They were about ten miles from a place named Goshen, when Bart saw a horse and buggy stopped beside the road half a mile ahead. Bart approached the buggy as Buster stayed back in the bushes. When he looked inside the buggy he saw a ladies purse and a satchel. He climbed in to grab the items, when someone yelled.

"Hey, what are you doing?"
Bart whirled to see a tall man running toward him.

"Get away from that buggy, mister." Said the man.

"Or what?" Bart replied.

"Or you'll get the blade of this shovel to the side of your head."

The man was carrying a shovel that he had been using to dig some wild asparagus roots.

"How about you stick that shovel in that big mouth of yours or I'll do it for you." Bart barked.

"Mister, around here we don't mess with other peoples' property." The man said as he approached Bart with the shovel raised shoulder level. Suddenly out of nowhere, Buster came flying in and slammed into the man from behind, knocking him to the ground. Bart grabbed the shovel that had flown out of the man's hand and proceeded to hit the man repeatedly in the head, until they heard the screams. They came from the far side of the ditch where a young girl was shrieking at them.

"Stop it! Stop it! You're going to kill him." The girl pleaded.

Bart yelled at Buster saying.

"Go get her Bull, and make sure she doesn't get away."

Bull ran across the road and down the ditch, but didn't realize how deep it was. He tumbled head first into the muck at the bottom of the ditch. When the girl saw Bull coming she turned and ran the opposite direction heading into the nearby woods. By the time Bull got up and managed to plod out of the muck, she was out of sight. Bull ran a ways into the woods but did not have a clue which way the girl had run. After walking for ten minutes, he looked around and panicked. He wasn't sure he could find his way out. He started yelling.

"Bart, where are you? Bart, where are you?" Bart yelled back.

"Over here. Over here."

When he finally found his way back to the wagon, Bart had already thrown the dead man into the ditch, and said to Bull.

"Did you get her?"

Bull, not wanting to disappoint his pal, paused and said.

"Yeah, uh, I took care-a-her."

Bart wondered why Bull hesitated when he answered, but chose to ignore it.

"We gotta get outa here.

Bart jumped into the buggy, and told Bull to get in. He figured there would be someone coming to look for this man and his kid when they didn't show up. They needed to put as much distance between them and the dead man as possible.

Chapter 3   Barbara

Barbara Miller was close to hysteria as she ran through the woods. She had heard the man with the shovel yell at the big guy to "Go get her, Bull." She saw the big lummox of a man running toward her and she ran. She was a fast runner and she knew these woods well as she often took a shortcut through them when going to her friend's house that was a mile from her house as the crow flies. If she took the roads it was more like two miles. She ran a half mile before stopping and listening. She heard nothing but the birds chirping. No footsteps, no twigs snapping. Then she heard one of them calling. At first she was petrified when she thought she heard.

"Barb, where are you? How did they know my name? Then she realized the big man was saying,

"Bart, where are you?"

She was terrified. The man she saw by their buggy had smashed her papa's head. She watched in horror as he just kept swinging the shovel. Then she heard an ear shattering scream come from the depths of her soul. The last thing that her father heard was his daughter's scream, before the last blow separated his spirit from his body.

Barbara stifled her sobs while looking over her shoulder.

She continued running toward her family's home. When she got to the back door she began crying loudly.

"Mama, mama," she cried, "oh mama." William, Nettie, and Lydia, her brother and two sisters, were the first to reach her.

"Barbara, what is wrong? Her younger brother said.

"Mama, mama." Barbara kept repeating. "Oh mama." Barbara collapsed on the floor. By this time Mary had come down from the upstairs and ran to Barbara.

"Barbara, what is the matter? What is wrong?"

"Ohhh no, mama. Ohhh nooo."
Her mother, Mary, was flustered now as she had never seen Barbara like this before.

"What happened, where is your papa?

"The man, and the big man are after me. He hit papa. He kept hitting papa."

Mary was scared now. A big man was after her? Were there two men? Mary ran into the back room and got the rifle that Jacob always kept on the wall rack. She took a cartridge from the drawer and pushed it into the chamber. She ran to the back door and looked out. There was no one out there. She ran to the front door and peered out to the road and saw that it too was clear. She went back to Barbara who had been helped onto the sofa by her brother and sisters.

"Barbara, you have to calm down. Where is your papa and when did this happen?"

"It was on the road over by Ganger's house. We were digging asparagus roots in the ditch. This man was going to steal our things and the buggy, and papa yelled at him and started to run to the buggy when this big man came out of nowhere and knocked papa down. Then the other man started hitting papa with the shovel. I think that is when I screamed and the big man saw me and started after me. I ran mama. I ran into the woods and I heard him coming. I thought he was going to kill me. Oh mama. He hurt papa bad."

Mary Miller was stunned. Her Jacob was hurt. Her oldest son, William, was only 10 years old. She had no one to protect the family if these men came after them. What could she do? She spoke to William and Lydia.

"I want both of you to run down to Schwartzwalter' house and have Mr. Schwartzwalter and his son come over here. Tell them that two men have hurt your papa and they may be coming to the house. Tell them to hurry. Barbara, go upstairs with Franklin. Do not wake him, but watch out the front window to see if you see the men coming. Nettie, you and I will watch for Susanna who will be coming home from work shortly. We will watch for her from the back of the house and warn her. Barbara, if you see anyone coming you yell for me."

An hour later, three neighbor men had taken Barbara to show them where this had happened. All the men were armed and ready to deal with any strangers that they met. They got to the area that Barbara said was where they had been digging asparagus. The men began searching the ditch. One of them moaned.

"Oh no. Over here." He cried.
The others gathered around the battered body of Jacob Miller that was partially submerged in the ditch. He was already cold to the touch. One man ran up to stop Barbara from coming down into the ditch.

"You don't want to see him this way, Barbara."
Barbara was silent and seemed stoic. She, however, was in a state of shock that would continue for a very long time.

Chapter 4   I Am Chauncey

My name is Chauncey Miller. That is pronounced Ch-awn-cee for those that need a guide for such things. I was born in 1864 and grew up in Elkhart County, Indiana near the town of Goshen. I have seven sisters and two brothers, all older than I. My mother has raised us almost by herself. My father, whom I never knew you see, was murdered before I was born. I did not even exist before he was taken from our family. I do remember that my sisters were unusually reluctant to discuss anything concerning our father when I would ask them when I was growing up.

I was not aware of the details concerning his death until two months ago. I confronted my sister, Barbara about my father. I asked her if he was a bad man since she had always avoided talking to me about him. I told her I had a right to know about my father, and then she started crying. After I said that, the floodgates opened. She told me that no, he was not bad; he was a very good man. He would help anyone. Then she sobbed more as she unfolded the entire trauma of that eventful day that happened twenty-three years ago. I had always been told that papa died before I was born. But neither my mother nor seven sisters or two brothers ever told me that my father died by the hands of another man.

What Barbara told me was the man who committed this act of violence was a drifter that was of large size, maybe six feet or more, skinny with dark black hair, and short scruffy facial hair that was likewise dark colored. She told me that she thought they were both very young, maybe four or five years older than she. Since this took place over twenty years prior, I have had hard times gaining information concerning these drifters. Since the day Barbara told me, I have had dreams of meeting this stranger. In stores, in bars, in town, on the road, and each time the same thing happened in the dream---he kills me. I have been feeling restless these last two month and feel that there is something I need to do. I just don't know what that is.

Barbara also told me that "black hair" was probably named Bart and traveled along with a large brute of a man whom he called Bull. Barbara remembered both names when they called back and forth to one another. She told me Bull was much bigger than Bart and had a large head. I have asked around the Goshen area, questioning the families that live within several miles of us but found no information about either of them. I decided that it was time to do some real detective work if I was to find leads on these two ogres, and satisfy my restlessness.

I recalled that Barbara told me the men had taken the horse and buggy after she had run away. I wondered what two fugitives would do with a horse and buggy that could be identified as the Millers'. Each buggy was hand made by a local craftsman, and could be easily identified. Some even had the family name carved in the undercarriage. I judged that the two would have sold it nearby but probably not in Goshen. I travelled to all of the local businesses in Goshen, asking owners if they ever remembered two strangers from twenty-three years ago. I usually got a laugh or an "are you kidding" response. Over a two week period I traveled to Nappanee, Wakarusa, Middlebury, Waterford, and Bristol. No one in these places remembered anything about the two men I described. There was a large livery in Elkhart, so I took a trip to visit them. I inquired about a horse and wagon that was sold twenty-three years ago and they laughed at me. I guess that meant that they did not remember that far back.

The livery was only two blocks from the train station in Elkhart so my mind again began to work. If these two characters sold the horse and buggy and wanted to leave town, the most logical means of leaving would be the train. I had no illusions of anyone in the train depot remembering two men buying train tickets twenty-three years ago, so once again I had hit a dead end. I left my horse at the livery and walked to the train station while I pondered these things. I had to start thinking like a fugitive. What would I do? Buy a ticket? Then what? Trains would not be sitting at the station waiting for me. No, I would buy the tickets and then probably go look for some food or drink.

I again set out on foot leaving the train station, heading north to the main street downtown area. The first place I saw that would have been a watering hole for the two scoundrels was a bar called Beer Belly's. I went in and ask the bartender if there was anyone that worked here twenty three years earlier. He told me that the bar didn't even exist then. I walked out and across the street was a place called Casey's. So I went in Casey's and found it to be a rather nice place inside. They served food as well as drinks. I walked up to the mahogany bar and asked the bartend.

"Do you know anyone that worked in here twenty-

three years ago?"
I got that same kind of look I got in the livery. An--- are you joking with me look. So I said.

"This is concerning two killers that may have come in here back then."
He replied.

"The owner is in the back. She has owned this place for at least thirty years. If you give me a minute, I'll see if she will talk to you."

The man went into the back room and my hopes seemed to dwindle that I would actually find out any information from that long ago. Several minutes passed and the bartend came out and told me the owner would be out in a minute.

The owner came out a minute later. She was a pleasant looking woman with grey wavy hair and piercing blue eyes. She was around 60 years of age. She introduced herself as Veronica Casey. I told her my name and the purpose for which I was asking these questions. She was very sympathetic to me and said.

"Let's go to the back room where we can talk in private."
She cleared off some papers from a table and motioned for me to take a seat at the table. She questioned me about the details of the two men who had killed my father.

I described the black haired man with the black scrubby facial hair who was named Bart, and traveled along with a very large man called Bull. I told her that my sister said they were both young, maybe eighteen or nineteen years old.

"Oh, and the Bull guy had a very large head." She thought for a moment and asked.

"Did the black haired man boss the big guy around?" I

replied to her.

"My sister told me that the black haired man, Bart, gave orders to the man named Bull to go after her."
She thought again. My heart actually gave a little skip as I thought this woman might really know something about them. She then narrated a story to me.

"I remember an incident long ago. Two young men came into the saloon and were having a drink at the bar. I was serving them and I recall that this black haired man was being rather braggadocios. He said he and his buddy were going to go out to Montana and were going to strike it rich mining gold. There was a man sitting beside him who just laughed and said something like; "you two are stupid for thinking you could get rich mining gold". Then this big guy that was with the black-haired man just went berserk. He picked the man up and threw him onto one of my tables and smashed it to smithereens. Then he proceeded to go after the man and started pummeling him with blows. That's when the black-haired guy went over to the big guy and calmly said 'Bull, that's enough.' And the big guy just stopped and walked away like nothing had ever happened. The black haired guy comes back to the bar smiles at me and says, 'He don't like being called stupid.' He slaps ten dollars on the bar and says, 'that's for the table and the drinks, keep the change.' Then the two of them just turned and walked out. I think that was twenty some years ago."

I was really excited. I think I have mined my first nugget of information. This had to be the same men. It fit the description that Barbara had given to me and the timing fits. The man named Bull was definitely subservient to the black-haired man. I intend to find out where these miscreants have gone.

Chauncey

Twenty-three years is a long time, and these two men could be anywhere in this country, or even dead, considering their hankering for violence. But a lead is a compass pointer that shows one which direction to take. I have determined that the direction that I will take is west to Montana. I will find my pa's killer. My pa left a void in my life that I shall never be able to recover. I don't even know the things that I missed without a father. There is a burning in my soul to find a conclusion to this murder that has troubled my family my entire life. The other thing is I have a hankering to travel and this seems like a good opportunity to satisfy that desire.

I walked back to the train depot and picked up some brochures about train times and destinations. I spent the next several days going to the local library looking up any stories I could find about mining areas out west. I looked through many months of papers from that period twenty years prior, and found that there were big gold strikes in both the Montana and Idaho territories. This was giving my restlessness some solid focus. The California gold fields, as far as the news reports, were all staked out in the 1860's, and the gold miners were looking for new strikes elsewhere. The biggest mining strikes back in the late 60's were in Virginia City, Butte, and Helena areas of Montana, and the Coeur d'Alene district of Idaho. The library had helped me narrow my point of interest. I need to do some planning.

My impulses are telling me where I need to go to pan for additional nuggets of information. Once a man has killed, it is likely that he will not become a preacher, or a law abiding citizen. He will most likely continue his immoral behavior. The memorials to his deeds will be indelibly etched in the minds of his victims or the witnesses. I have already discovered that even twenty-three years does not diminish memories of evil when it is witnessed. Consequently, I will have a somewhat hazy roadmap of tidbits to decipher in pursuance of the black-haired man, Bart, and his partner named Bull.

Chapter 5   The Travelling

I have obtained some maps from the local general store and gone back to the Goshen library also to study the areas to which I planned to travel. I have learned as much as possible about the Helena, Billings and Virginia City areas of Montana. From what I read it seems that they are all very lawless territories and possibly dangerous for a greenhorn like myself. The only train line to that part of Montana is called the Northern Pacific. I must travel to St. Paul, Minnesota in order to connect with that railroad.

I have talked to my family about this and ma is not in favor of me leaving. She does not want me hunting for pa's killers. She said it is too dangerous and it was too long ago. She told me losing one family member is enough. Those scoundrels will never be found. I did not tell her of the lead I had discovered in the Elkhart bar. My older brother, Franklin was very interested in my story. Franklin is two years older than I, but has no memory of the incident. He also was never told that papa was murdered, but he did remember the agony the family went through in the ensuing years. I told him what I found out from Barbara, and then about the trip to Elkhart. He wants to help find the murderers. We sat down together and made plans. Franklin and I will travel together and seek more information wherever we go; to try and fill the void that we both have felt growing up without a father.

Two weeks later, we packed as many of our belongings as could be managed, into two large grips and found that they were too heavy for us to carry. I had to go through and eliminate the things that would not be absolutely necessary. I removed two books other than the Bible, which I had desired to have for reading on the train and in hotels on the way to our destination. The two books were by Longfellow, my favorite author, "The Song of Hiawatha" and "Tales of a Wayside Inn." This lightened my load by several pounds. We still needed to rid more items. After much angst, Franklin took out a pair of heavy boots, a large overcoat and a few tools that he thought would be needed. I did however keep my Colt Single Action Army .45 caliber revolver. Two boxes of .45 caliber ammunition weighed almost five pounds so I removed one of the boxes of 25 cartridges. We decided that once we got out west we could buy whatever other weapons that we thought we would need. Franklin said to me.
"Chauncey, if we do find these men, what are we planning to do to them? Do you think that you would shoot them?"
I thought about that for a long time.
"I don't know what I'll do when we find them. I think we need to have a list of ideas in mind before we stumble into a fight with those two."

Once the two grips were reduce to manageable weights, the time for buying our tickets on this mission was now a reality. When I walked outside, the world looked different to me. Reality hit me square in the face. No longer was I thinking in terms of my life here on the farm in Indiana. The sky looked bluer than I remember it ever looking. The birds were singing louder than they normally sang. My family seemed dearer to me. I realized that I was leaving the only way of life that I had ever known. I had never been more than twenty miles from our house. My friends, most of which were relatives and neighbors, would be left behind. My world was about to turn over a new leaf. Whether that would be a good or a bad thing, I could not foresee. The unknown that lay before me was a scary world indeed.

Franklin and I hitched up our horse and wagon and drove to the train depot in Elkhart to purchase the tickets. We were both unusually quiet on the thirty minute trip. We both felt the upcoming change as one feels a change in weather coming. The dark clouds were on the horizon. Stormy, calm, lightning, or wind; we were heading right into it.

The tickets to Chicago were three dollars each and departed Elkhart two days hence. Once in Chicago the other tickets would be purchased for Chicago - St.Paul in order to get to the Northern Pacific Railroad. Our excitement was great with the anticipation of this journey into the unknown. We had excited discussions on the trip home. We were going to Chicago, one of the largest cities in America. The clouds didn't look so ominous now; there was the promise of adventure. As our wagon approached the house we both let out a WHHHOOOOOP! Three of our sisters ran from the house to see what was the matter.
"What are you whooping about?" They asked.
"We're finally getting away from the seven of you" I said.

Franklin and I had a good laugh about that. Our sisters no longer all lived in the house. Three of them were married and had children. They had all built houses on our property and their husbands farmed our land. William, our oldest brother, was also married and had built an addition on the back of our house where he, his wife, and his three boys lived. William was very much supportive of our trip, even though he would be losing two helpers on the farm. William wanted us to bring justice to the two men who had killed our father.

The next two nights we sat around in the evenings and had long discussions about the future. What do we do when or if we do find the two murderers? We had no good answer to that one. What if we get out to the gold mining area and happen to get lucky and strike it rich? There was a long discussion on that one involving moving to California, building a big mansion, and finding two fine looking women to marry. What happens if we get lost and are kidnapped by Indians? In point of fact, we both were very nervous about this trip and what the final resolution would be. We finally decided that the planning and preparation for a trip was probably the best part, what might happen was in the hands of God.

Chapter 6 Farewell

There was not a dry eye amongst the assemblage of brothers, sisters, mother, nephews, nieces and assorted cousins on the morning we departed. There were more people at the house than there was at a normal church service. There were many goodbyes and well wishes. Even our neighbor Franklin Logan, had come over to wish us well. I noticed that he spent a lot of time talking to our sister Nettie. Oh well, he was a good man and a hard worker. There were few single men left in the area to marry our remaining single sister. All of the other sisters had depleted the available pool of bachelors.

William took us by buggy to the train station that early spring morning. Franklin and I boarded the train in Elkhart after getting a big bear hug from our brother and an admonition from him to watch for trouble behind us, because it never comes at you head on.

Franklin got the window seat and we were on our way to

Chicago. After an hour or so of traveling we saw some tremendous sand dunes on the north side of the train and then got glimpses of the huge lake that we had only read about: Lake Michigan. It was magnificent and larger than we had ever imagined. Then we saw the buildings of Chicago in the distance. The largest building I had ever seen was the five story hotel in Elkhart. There were buildings in Chicago everywhere that dwarfed the Elkhart hotel.

We stood in amazement when we got off of our train in Union Depot. There were people and buildings all around us. Never had we been around so many people, even at one of our Stutzman- Miller family reunions. We asked one of the conductors where we could buy a ticket to St. Paul, Minnesota and he pointed to a booth about fifty yards away. When we got to the booth the ticket agent told us that the next train to St. Paul would leave at 6:00 am the next morning. He was very nice to us and informed us of a good place to stay overnight.

We took our grips and walked following the directions he had given us. The hotel was several blocks away on a street called LaSalle. On the way there, two young girls approached us and asked us if we wanted some company. Franklin blushed. I figured that our money would be in danger if those two were within arm's reach of our pockets. I said.
        "No thanks we're meeting our wives." As they walked away, Franklin said
        "Were they — ?"
        "Yes they were," I replied.

That was our introduction to the big city. We could only hope the rest of our journey would be as friendly. We ate that evening at the Rock Island Train Station in a place called a

Cafeteria, where we could choose from an assortment of food such as we had never seen. The food was lined up on a platform that was twenty feet long. We could pick any type of food you could imagine from asparagus to zucchini and meat dishes from Angus beef to venison. Needless to say we were completely stuffed by the end of the evening. The total price for the humongous meal was one dollar.

After a restless night, we arose early around 4:00 am, as neither of us had slept well in the strangeness of the city. There is a lot of noise in the big city. Based on our encounter the previous day, we decided that the money we were carrying needed to be in more than one place. We both stashed money in several places on our person and in our grips. At least we wouldn't lose it all at once. The train was on time at the Union Depot and our journey resumed on the way to St. Paul at 6:05.

Chapter 7   Virginia City

Bart and Buster were enjoying some modicum of success after ten years in Virginia City, Montana. Bart had obtained a one- half interest in a saloon that was the 'go to' spot in this Wild West city, where lawlessness was celebrated every evening. Virginia City was a booming town when the gold fever hit. People flooded in from the West California gold fields and from the East as far as Boston. The city had a population of 10,000 when Bart and Bull arrived. Of the entire population, there may have been a handful of law abiding citizens, but the thing was: there were no laws to obey.   There was gunfire, robbing, and murder on a daily basis. Were you a timorous person, it was guaranteed that sooner more than later you would be the victim of one of these transgressions.

Bart was not a timid person. He was confrontational, and took advantage of any situation in which he perceived he was dominant. Ninety percent of those situations that Bart asserted his authority were when Bull was by his side. Bull went unchallenged in Virginia City. People were just not that stupid. Bull was now a full grown man of six foot seven inches height, and a weight of 300 lbs. He was strong and he was fast. But without a challenger, he was stagnating. His physical skills were not honed to the level that they had been ten years prior but he seemed to be smarter than Bart remembered him at age thirteen.

The reason that Bull currently went unchallenged had to do with an event that occurred two years after their arrival in Virginia City. There was a man by the name of "The Deacon" who was feared throughout the region. He was a claim jumper and all around troublemaker. He practiced the art of stealing claims or coercing miners to sell their claims for small sums of money when they ran out of supplies. The way he did this was with a group of hired hands that would be his strong arm in persuading miners to sell or else; "else" meaning physical harm or death.

Once gold was found on a claim, The Deacon would send his men to the claim owner and offer to buy his claim from him. If the miner was reluctant to "sell" his claim, they would be convinced to sell by physical threats, beatings, or in some cases the miner would just disappear. The Deacon could easily forge the miners signature on a bill of sale, since most of them couldn't write their own names, they signed with an "X." He would take ownership of their claim, thus "jumping" onto their land and setting up a large sluicing operation that was much quicker and more efficient than a single individual panning a claim by hand.

The Deacon was brutal and was known to make miners disappear quicker than a man could down a mug of beer. There were no appeals, local law enforcement or courts of law that a miner could turn to when their claims were jumped. The Deacon was the law unto himself. He was a gunslinger with a very stout exterior, approaching Bull in size, almost, but not quite. He also was rumored to be one of the leaders in the Henry Plummer gang, a notorious gang that robbed and killed in the Virginia City area. The Deacon could be described in two words: ruthless and frightening.

Bart and Bull had not had initial success in mining. After a year they received some advice from an old codger that recommended a specific area in Alder Gulch. They ended up mining an area in a very productive site south of Virginia City, along the Alder Gulch Creek. They began panning the creek, and within a week had found a significant quantity of gold nuggets and filed an official claim. When The Deacon got wind of the "strike" by Bart, he sent his group of men out immediately to "convince" Bart that he would be much better off and easily make more money if he sold the claim to them.

That is when The Deacon's men first met Bull. Bull had been sleeping in the shade of their wagon under some cottonwood trees by the creek's edge. Bull had done some heavy digging for over twelve hours and was exhausted. He awoke when he heard the raised voices of men threatening Bart. He strode down to the creek where Bart was standing surrounded by three of The Deacon's men. Bull saw The Deacon's men start to move toward Bart. He yelled at them.
        "Hey, you boys got a problem?"
The Deacon's men turned to see a mountain of a man coming toward them. Their demeanor immediately changed and they decided the best course of action would be to leave.

When word got back to The Deacon of what had transpired, he knew he had to confront the situation because his reputation was at stake. He went looking for Bart and Bull. He found them in the Spur Saloon the following day. Gossip had already spread that The Deacon was looking for Bart and Bull the two men that had scared away The Deacon's men.

People always loved to see a good fight. The local undertaker especially loved a good fight because he benefitted no matter who won. People began to line up outside the Spur, peering into the windows and doors to get a glimpse of the confrontation.

The Deacon with four of his men, walked into the Spur and people inside scattered. Bart and Bull were standing at the bar having a drink. The Deacon spoke first.

"BART DECKER!" He bellowed. "My men tell me that you threatened them and chased them away from a public area."

Bart and Bull turned slowly and Bart replied.

"That 'public area' belongs to me and Bull. We have an official claim on that land and if you don't keep your men away from me, the next time you'll find them floating face down in the creek if they threaten me."

"Big words for a little man!" Laughed The Deacon.

Then Bull spoke in a booming voice.

"Mister, you keep away from us and you stay offa our claim or I'll squash you like the bug that you are."

The Deacon's men looked at Deacon and at one other. They had no desire to challenge this bear of a man. They took a step back away from The Deacon. Then Deacon spoke.

"Decker, you and me are gonna go outside and settle this like real men settle a spat."

Bull, spit on the floor and sneered.

"Lick my spit you slimy, gutless weasel."

The Deacon laughed.

"Whatsa matter little Bart, you have to have your boy speak for you?"

Bull stepped toward Deacon and his men took another step backward.

"I ain't his boy you shitfaced coward. You have somthin to say to Bart, you say it to me. You understand?"

This is when The Deacon's men detected a small hint of reluctance in him. He hesitated, before he said.

"Then you and me'll step outside and we'll see if your actions are as big as your words."

The two huge men stepped out into the dusty street, while eager onlookers quickly set up refuge behind whatever obstacles they could find. This could be the best fight they had seen in months. The Deacons men being no less fearsome of the impending melee took refuge also. Bull strode unflinchingly out into the middle of the street while the Deacon began noticing that his men had surreptitiously deserted him. Bull pulled back his long overcoat behind his revolver holster glaring without a blink at his adversary. Bull retorted.

"Movin a little slow Deacon?" To which Deacon replied.

"Just makin sure you don't have no one bushwhacking me out here."

Bull chortled.

"My ma delivered me faster than it took you got out here Deacon. Let's get this over, I'm getting hungry."

As Deacon slowly took a position about fifteen feet in front Bull, there were visible beads of sweat forming on his brow. He knew he could not back down from this confrontation or his reputation would be shattered. He did not know if Bull was quick on the draw or not. He was worried however, that if he did outdraw this giant, and hit him with the first shot---it most likely would not knock him down. It would more than likely just make him mad. That is what was causing the beads of sweat to concentrate and run down his temples.

Deacon had never been in a gunfight where he drew first. He always prided himself in letting the other guy make the first move. This time he broke his own rule. He made the first move.

Bull was no rookie with a gun. He had practiced many hours in front of a mirror and best of all against Bart, who was very fast. He could beat Bart every time. Of course that was without ammunition and it was just playing around. This was no longer playing around. But the one thing that Bull didn't have that Deacon did have---was fear.

Bull saw it in Deacon's eyes; his fear was palpable. Then Bull saw Deacon twitch and knew that he was making his move. In one fluid motion Bull swung his hand upwards as he snatched his gun from the holster, raised it, leveled it and pulled the trigger. The Deacon had just begun to raise his gun when he knew that it hadn't been nearly fast enough. The .45 caliber bullet struck him in the right shoulder of his drawing arm. It spun him around almost 180 degrees as his gun went off harmlessly, his bullet hitting the ground five feet in front of Bull. The Deacon hit the ground with a thud and a cloud of dust. There was an audible gasp from the crowd of onlookers. The Deacon would rise again from the dust and live, but his reputation would forever be in the dirt. The Bull had acquired that reputation the second he reholstered his gun.

Chapter 8   Ghost Dance

 F ranklin and I had travelled as far as Mandan, North

Dakota on the Northern Pacific Railroad. We spent our days looking at the scenery of large fields of grain pass by us as we rode the rails through Minnesota. We had been amazed at the breadth of the mighty Mississippi. The biggest river we had ever seen was the Elkhart River that was small enough I could throw a stone across it.

We passed through miles and miles of uninhabited plains in western Minnesota and North Dakota and were impressed by their vastness. But now, the train had been delayed in Mandan, North Dakota because of an early spring blizzard that had dropped over a foot of snow east of Miles City, Montana into the western parts of North Dakota. They told us there were drifts of three to four feet deep across the entire area that made a train crossing impossible. The only option was for us to wait for the snows to melt before proceeding. They told us to plan on waiting about a week.

We had read in the newspapers of the infamous Hunkpapa Lakota Sioux "Ghost Dance" that had been widely spreading throughout all of the Indian tribes. It was a mystic by the name Wavoka that had seen a vision during a solar eclipse which occurred on the first day of the New Year in January of 1889. The vision was a spiritual revelation that told him that all Indians must love rather than fight, should neither lie nor steal and should not practice self mutilation in mourning the dead. They believed that if all Indians followed these rules: they would be reunited with their families from the afterlife, the white man would be driven from their lands, and the mighty buffalo herds would return to their lands once again.

One of these "Ghost Dances" or "circle dances" was taking place on the large Standing Rock Indian Reservation only thirty miles south of Mandan. I wanted to see this phenomenon that was occurring at the reservation as I had read in the newspapers. I convinced Franklin to take a stagecoach ride with me down to the Standing Rock Reservation to see for ourselves this mystic dance that was sweeping the Indian Nations.

We boarded the stagecoach that travelled south along the Missouri river with a destination of Fort Pierre, in South Dakota. Fort Pierre was the main stopping point for miners that passed through on their way west to the Black Hills gold fields in the early 1870's. We told the driver that we wanted to get off of the stage at an Indian village near a place called Half Timber Butte. This was one of the larger villages of the Lakota Sioux tribe in all of the Standing Rock Reservation. It was a large flatland area west of the Missouri river that continued ten miles west to the Half Timber Butte. The Indians considered the Butte area to be a sacred site because from this camp in the summer months, the sun would set or disappear behind the Butte.

The stagecoach driver strongly advised us not to get off the stage at this point. The driver told us we could not trust those redskins. He said.

"They'll kill you, scalp you, and then eat your innards. Besides, the next coach won't come through here for two days. They won't find nothin but your bare bones bakin in the sun." I laughed at him and told him.

"I mean no harm to them, so why would they want to hurt us?"

The stagecoach driver shook his head.

"You younguns will find out these savages don't care if you are the Great White Chief or a lowly farmer. They consider us white folks to all look the same: when our scalps are removed."

With that, the stagecoach left us behind in a cloud of dust. Franklin looked out over the hundreds of teepees that graced the vast flat grassland in front of us. He had never seen such a view of Indians, teepees, and vacant land with nothing but grass and scrub brush. We walked toward the village of teepees where we heard what sounded like a hundred horses stomping their hooves in unison and a soulful wailing.

I saw him first as we approached the circle of teepees. An Indian dressed in full battle garb, with white and red streaked face paint, a headband with two large eagle feathers, bare chest, a necklace strung with large bear claws, a loin cloth with dangling tassels and a tomahawk in his hand approached us. He spoke very good English.

"What does the white man want? You come to make laughter at the Indian's dancing?"

Franklin replied.

"We have no ill intent; we are interested in your Ghost Dance. We too saw the darkening of the sun on the first day of this year, and wondered what the sacred meaning of the sun and moon coming together foretold."

This was the best thing that he could have said. In one short statement he had let the Indian know that we were interested in their Ghost Dance, the significance of the sun (eclipse), and how that was a sacred happening in their culture.

The brave said to me and my brother.
        "Follow me."
We were escorted to a central area that was encircled by a wall of teepees. In the middle was a large fire with hundreds of young and old braves encircling it. They danced in a rhythm of bending and strutting punctuated by a throbbing beat of elk skin drums of which there were at least twenty. The vibrations from the drums were so great they would shake your very innards.

The dancing braves, circled in a counter clockwise direction with two to three braves side by side. They chanted as they stomped their feet, matching the drum beats. There was another circle of older men that surrounded the braves in an outer circle that went clockwise around the inner circle. The harmony of the chanting seemed to have been that of an accomplished choir. It was melodious and very inspiring to listen to.

We could not speak as the spectacle that we saw was truly awesome. Speaking was not a viable option, as we would have been unable to hear one another anyway.

The dance went on for many hours. As the fire burned down to a pile of glowing embers the drums and the chanting abruptly halted. One man with a long headdress of dozens of eagle feathers that extended to his waist, made a wailing cry similar to a wolves howl. He danced alone around the embers all the while emitting warbling howls. Just as suddenly as the Ghost Dance had stopped; he stopped. A brave threw a long spear toward him that stuck in the ground at the man's feet. The brave pulled the spear from the ground and swept it through the glowing embers once, twice then a third time. He then raised the spear in both hands above his head and walked barefooted into the embers. I heard Franklin gasp. The brave made no noise as he slowly walked across the embers that were at least ten feet across. When he completed his fire walk, there was a cacophony of yelps and whoops from the surrounding crowd.

The yelps and whoops were not coordinated as the dancing had been. It was a short-lived celebration of the success of the lone warriors walk through fire that symbolized the tribe's trials.

It was later explained to us that the fire signified all of the trials that the Lakota had faced: the spotted fever sickness, the wars with competing tribes, the wars with the white soldiers, and the thousands of Indians that had gone to the afterlife since the white man came. The raised spear represented the tribes that were being lifted out of the fires of the Indian's trials and carried through to deliverance into their redemption on the other side.

The circle dance around the fire was the connection between their old way of life and the present. The counter rotating circles of braves were the confusion that they faced between the old ways and the new lives that they faced in a white man's world. The "Ghost Dance" was to beseech the Creator, to bring back the old ways of the tribes. Life before the white man: honesty, harmony, no wars, no killing, reunion with those in the afterlife and the return of the buffalo herds that had been decimated.

As the first light of dawn began to show on the horizon, all activity abruptly halted. It was as if a band leader waved their arms to stop them. The people all dissolved away into the teepees. Franklin and I looked at one other as if to say; what do we do now. We were both dead tired even though we had only been spectators and not participants in the dancing. The brave that had brought us into the camp came up to me and said.

"Was your spirit moved by the circle dance?"
I replied.

"We did feel a connection with mother earth that we have not felt before."
The brave said to us.

"My name is "Screaming Eagle. I am the medicine man of the Lakota Sioux. I will take you to a teepee where you can rest."

"My name is Chauncey, and this is my brother Franklin. We have come from far away in search of a white man who killed our father."
Screaming Eagle said.

"Take it from an old man who knows. You will never find peace from seeking revenge as it only passes vengeance on to the next generation.

He took us to a teepee on the outer edge of the circle. We were given two soft buffalo hides to lie on. Within minutes we were both sound asleep. Sometime later, I am not sure how long we had slept, but I awoke with a start. There was a young boy, of around five or six years of age, standing inside our teepee, staring at us. When I jerked awake he fled the teepee and I heard him and his friends outside, laughing.

I picked up the buffalo hide and put it over my head and walked through the doorway. When the children saw me they laughed even harder. I put my hands on either side of my head and pointed my index fingers into the air imitating bull horns. I bent forward at the waist and swung my head from side to side and pawed at the ground with my foot. The children were now really into the game I was playing. They imitated bows and arrows being strung and shot at me. When they released their fictitious arrows, I swooned to the side and fell on my back and put my feet and arms in the air. The children fell down with laughter. Some of the adults nearby were now watching intently at this crazy white man that was playing with their children. Some of them also began laughing and pointing at me.

Screaming Eagle came up to me and told me that the Chief would like see us. I got up and brushed myself off and woke Franklin who was still in a sound sleep. We followed Screaming Eagle to a teepee that had four smaller teepees around it. Screaming Eagle motioned for us to follow him into the teepee. Upon entering, the Chief, who had been sitting by a small fire in the center, rose and greeted us.

"I am Chief Big Foot. Screaming Eagle has told me how you have amused our young ones. I am happy to meet men who are humble enough to enjoy entertaining our children. Please sit with me and we will pass the peace pipe."

Franklin and I introduced ourselves, and sat along with Screaming Eagle and Chief Big Foot. While we sat and passed the peace pipe to one another, Chief Big Foot spoke.

"Screaming Eagle tells me you are searching for two men that killed your father"
Franklin replied.

"This was many years ago when we were both very young. We only found out that our father was killed several months ago. The men we are looking for were said to have come out west to search for wealth in the gold fields."

"I had a vision last night about the men that you seek." Screaming Eagle said.

"The men you seek are not now where they once were. They were driven from their homes and have moved on to a new village. They are not together at this time. One man lives among his friends and is no longer the man he used to be. The other one lives in the hills among much wealth. There is much of what he seeks near him. He has not changed his ways, but continues to live by preying on others."

Chief Big Foot then told us that he wanted us to accompany a hunting party that was to leave the camp in a hunt for tatanka (which is buffalo). Screaming Eagle took us to the edge of camp where there were approximately fifteen braves on horseback. They brought us two horses that had no saddles. Neither Franklin nor I had ridden bareback before, but we had both ridden horses often, back on the farm.

We mounted the horses with some difficulty since there were no stirrups to help get on. Screaming Eagle went along with us but told us he usually did not go with the hunting party, he was there to translate for us, since the others did not speak our language. While we were still struggling to get on the horses, the hunting party rode off. By the time we were ready, the entire hunting party was a quarter mile ahead of us.

"They aren't real excited about us coming along with them, are they?" I said to Screaming Eagle.
He looked at me but did not reply. I knew the answer. We rode for almost an hour heading in a southwesterly direction. We passed to the south of Half Timber Butte and saw another

butte to the west and another to the south. Screaming Eagle told us that in the old days the buffalo herds would come through this land between the buttes and would cover the entire area which was fifteen to twenty miles wide. I could not imagine that many animals covering the entire ground. He told us the sound of the giant herd could be heard all the way to the "Great River" which was the Missouri. We were now twenty miles from the river. But when we looked over the plains; there was not a single buffalo in sight. Screaming Eagle told us that the buffalo would graze on the vast grasslands that were along the river. They would migrate from the grasslands that lay to the north and west, and as the massive herd depleted the food, they would follow the river to a better area. There were few places that they could cross the river that meandered from the northwest, so this was a good land to hunt.

He said now that he was old; the herd had dried up as he had dried up.

"They no longer are what they were in my youth as I am no longer what I was back then."
Franklin asked him why we were continuing when there were no buffalo in sight.

"One of our scouts saw a small herd out near what is called Piuss Butte yesterday. It is another ten miles. We will be there when the sun is overhead."
None of us spoke for a long while. We began to understand the predicament that the Indian tribes were in as they had been placed on a reservation and could no longer migrate with the great buffalo herds like they did in the past. The great herds were gone. So were the once proud Indian tribes.

The hunting party halted about the time Screaming Eagle had predicted. The sun was directly overhead. One of the hunters pointed in the distance to the south of us where I saw a herd of maybe one or two hundred buffalo grazing. The leader motioned to several of his men to go to the west side of the herd and the rest of us rode to the east.

I soon saw that the herd was getting restless. They broke into two groups and started moving further south. They were not running, but they were moving slowly away from us. The initial hunting party that the leader had sent out was riding quickly to the herd's back side. We were approaching more slowly to the opposite side of the herd. When our two hunting groups were almost directly across from one another; the group on the far side let out a spine tingling howl of yelling and whooping, riding directly at the herd.

The herd turned from the noise and started running straight toward us. Our group spread out and waited for the small herd to come by. The herd leader sensed something wrong as they approached us. He must have been a wise old bull as he again turned and led the herd to the south away from us. Our leader charged after them in pursuit. The lead buffalo were already out of range of the rifles, but there were older and slower buffalo that lagged behind, and those were the ones that our party was able to bring down. They were only able to shoot ten or twelve of the group we had seen. The rest easily escaped.

Screaming Eagle told us that in his youth on such a hunting party, there would be sixty or seventy buffalo taken. That would be enough to supply the tribe food and clothing for many months. The few buffalo we had taken today would only feed the tribe for several weeks.

"Some of our tribes are starving. The buffalo are no longer numerous enough to feed us. The cattle ranches surrounding us let their cattle roam and diminish the grassland for the remaining buffalo. The soldiers do not bring us the beef that they promised when we were put on the reservation. They told us to grow crops that will sustain us for the entire year. We do not have the people that know how to cultivate this land to grow crops. The circle dance is our last hope to restore our lands to the way they were."

Both Franklin and I were speechless. We had so much back at our home in Indiana and didn't realize it. We had fertile land to grow crops. We had cows to supply us with milk; steers to provide meat, and markets where we could purchase what we couldn't grow. None of this was available out here. We both had a helpless feeling for the plight of these people.

The white man's greed and selfishness had actually changed a way of life that would soon become extinct. We returned to the camp without another word being spoken. Screaming Eagle and Big Foot had shown us what words could never relate the hopeless plight that lay ahead for a nation in captivity. This lesson was to stay with me the rest of my life.

Chapter 9   The Deacon

Bart had become exactly like his old nemesis. The men that formerly worked for The Deacon, now worked for Bart. Bull did not like nor did he agree with what Bart was doing. Bart Decker was feared for his ruthlessness much as The Deacon had been. He stole, robbed, and plundered those that were afraid to confront him. That was everyone: except Bull. Arguments became frequent between the two old friends. Bull would tell him he was becoming just like Deacon. Bart's reply was;

"Bull, if you don't like all of the money we have. You are free to pursue your own course of action."

Lawlessness in Virginia City and all areas of the Montana territory was rampant. The common folk were fed up with being intimidated by the entire criminal element. There was a movement that had begun to address this. They called themselves the "Vigilance Committee." Their goal was to intimidate the intimidators. It was mob mentality. But it worked. More and more lawless men were being dealt justice via a tree limb on the end of a rope.

In a one month period in the mid 1860's, more than twenty lawless criminals were hanged by the Montana Vigilantes. The lawless element was becoming concerned and fearful. Somehow these vigilantes knew who they were, and where they lived. The scales of justice and intimidation had tipped and gone to the opposite extreme.

One of the intimidation tactics of the Montana Vigilantes was a code that they used. A probable criminal would either be hung if they were "worthy" or given a warning if suspected of wrongdoing. The criminal/undesirable would find a cryptic note left on their doorway. The note was simply "**3-7-77**."

No one knew for sure what the numbers meant. Some thought that it meant the dimensions of a grave — 3 feet wide, 7 feet long, and 77 inches deep. Whatever it meant; the criminals learned that it doomed them to a stretched neck it they did not leave town in the following twenty-four hours. The smart criminals fled, the stupid ones died.

Bart Decker found such a note on his doorway one morning in late fall. He panicked. He ran to Bull's room and said.

"Bull. The Vigilantes have warned us to get out of town. I got the note on my door this morning."

"Was there a note on my door?" Bull asked.

"No, there wasn't one on your door, but they know you-n-me are partners."

"Are we? I don't see no fancy things in my room that you have at your place"

"Come on Bull. You know I share everything with you. What's mine is yours. We have always done everything tagether. We have ta leave."

"What if I don't wanna leave, Bart? What are ya gonna do then?"

"Come on Bull. You and me go back a long ways. We do things together. We always have."

Bull was becoming bolder now. He never feared Bart. He just felt he needed his friendship---now he wasn't sure if he did.

"Bart, I ain't the one that shot that banker. I didn't beat no man to death with a shovel, and I ain't lied and cheated people out of their land out here. So now you want me to help you get outa here?"

"Bull, they're gonna hang us if we don't leave. They don't care what you done. They know you are my partner and they'll hang you too. Get your stuff together; we need to leave by tonight."

Bull looked at Bart like he didn't know who he was. Indeed Bull was not the same man he was when they left Kentucky. He had been young, stupid and trusting of his friend. His only friend. Since that time, Bull had thought a lot about the things that Bart had done, that he was being blamed for. Things that he had never done. It was Bart that was the murderer, thief and robber. Not him! But he realized he was guilty by being Bart's partner. He decided he needed to leave this time. But, this was the last time Bart would be his partner.

That evening Bart and Bull with all of their worldly belongings in packs on four horses, mounted their horses and rode off to the north. Bart had gone to the half owner of their saloon and offered to sell him his half for a thousand dollars. Bart told him that is one-fourth of what it is worth. The other man sensing that Bart was in some kind of trouble offered him five hundred. Bart took it.

"Where we headed?" Bull asked.

"Figured we could head up to Missoula. Heard there's some good livin up there."

Bull grunted.

"I ain't doing no more mining and no more intimidating Bart. I'm done. You and I get to Missoula. You go your way and I go mine."

The problem was: Bart and Bull never got to Missoula. After a week of travel they were following a trail that went through the hills to the west of Butte. They were planning to follow the trail north until they reached the Hellgate River which would lead them to Missoula. A snow storm hit them hard. The snow was too heavy to continue. They were stranded and had no idea where they were exactly. Bull set about building a lean-to shelter. Bart went about finding kindling dry enough to start a fire. Their survival depended on both. The snow was not letting up it was getting heavier and the wind was picking up.

They were able to build a substantial shelter made of pine boughs. Bull wisely built the shelter under heavy cover of some large pine trees that gave them additional cover from the raging blizzard of snow. In the front of the shelter they were able to coax a fire started and heat some cans of beans. Their four pack horses and two riding horses were tied to a line they attached between two nearby small trees. That night they heard wolves howling very nearby. Bart got out his rifle and Bull had his pistol handy in case the wolves got any closer. It was a restless night with the horses uneasy due to the howling wolves. Bart and Bull alternated sleeping in two hours shifts, while the other kept watch.

The following morning, they found out that the howling had not all been wolves. The snow had let up and they could see movement among the trees surrounding their shelter. The movement was not four legged animals. It was Blackfoot Indians. About ten of them.
Bart called out.
  "Hello. We are friends. We mean no harm."
No reply.

"Can you hear us? We have things to trade you.
No reply. Bart said to Bull.
"What should we do?"

  Bull stood up and walked out of the shelter plodding
through the deep snow directly toward the nearest man that
was visible. The Indian saw him coming and raised his rifle,
pointing it toward the oncoming Bull. Bull held both arms
high in the air and stopped walking. Six Indians came out of
the shadows and surrounded Bull. Others stayed hidden and
alert. One of the Blackfoot spoke broken English.
  "What want in trade?"
He wondered what the two crazy white men had to trade
them. Bull and Bart had an assortment of pots and pans,
mirrors, knives and extra guns that would be of interest to the
Blackfoot men. Would they live long enough to trade, was the
question?

Chapter 10   Tatanka

 F ranklin and I spent the night back at the Standing Rock camp in the teepee talking about the things that we had seen. We had watched the skillful hunters butcher the tatanka (buffalo), saving as much as possible for their needs. Some of the bones were taken for making stays to hold the hides together on teepees, the skull and horns were used ornamentally in ceremonies, the meat of course was being dried for food, some of the entrails were used as water carriers, others had medicinal uses that our medicine man explained to us. All in all, there were only a few bare bones of the carcasses left when they were done.

When we arrived back in camp, there was a greeting party to meet us, excited to see what was brought back. The squaws immediately took the buffalo hides and began the preparations to scrape, stretch and dry them for clothing and teepee covers. The children were given the livers that were a delicacy that they chewed raw.

That evening we had a feast of tatanka meat roasted over an open fire. It was the first time either Franklin or I had ever tasted buffalo. The meat was delicious. Screaming Eagle asked us many questions about our plans after we left. We told him that we were going to travel to Bozeman and then

Butte Montana to check the mining areas there for anyone that knew of the men called Bart and Bull.

Then Franklin held up his finger and waved it at Screaming Eagle.

"You have shown us all of this for a reason, haven't you? The Ghost Dance, the fire walk, the hunting party: all of that was to provide us with a message."

Screaming Eagle said,

"You must seek more than the trail of these two men; otherwise you will be in search of ghosts for the rest of your lives. Seek happiness and what will fulfill you in your lives. Seeking an evil presence will often lead one to harmful spirits. To attract good spirits you must seek positive thoughts and deeds. Our people have been wounded in spirit from many years of hate and anger. We have done nothing but seek revenge on the white man for his wrongdoing to our people. You have seen for yourself the condition of my people as a result of this negative thinking. We starve to death and cannot feed ourselves. We seek to count coup on the white man blaming him for our misfortune, and in doing so we foolishly abandon our humanity. Our warriors no longer have the pride and honor that they had when they were the valiant hunters bringing food and clothing back from battle with the tatanka. We have shamed our true identity. We live within the boundaries of a reservation that is a glorified prison camp that cannot possibly accommodate our needs. Your lesson is what you take from here when you leave. How do you think your lives will be any different if you seek revenge for the anger that you feel? Only a bad destiny can result from a mission of revenge. Seek to support those that mistreat you and your life will be fulfilled. If you exist only to destroy others, you will destroy yourself."

Chapter 11   Blackfoot

The Blackfoot Indians took Bart and Bull and their pack horses on a trail that led down the mountain from the higher elevation. The going was slow and treacherous. However, within a half-hour the snowfall had diminished to flurries and the depth of the snow was now only six or eight inches. When they came into a flat area in another hour, there was only an inch or two of snow.   They travelled in a northeasterly direction for the remainder of the day, arriving in the Blackfoot camp after darkness had fallen. Curiosity brought most of the camp out to meet the raiding party. Bull noticed a very beautiful dark haired squaw that was looking at him. When he met her eyes with his, she looked away. Bart and Bull were not tied up, but they were closely guarded during the night.

The following morning Bull and Bart were awakened by one of the braves from the raiding party that had brought them in. He motioned for them to follow him. They were taken to a wrinkled man who appeared very old but had much wisdom in his eyes. He spoke to them.

"I am known as Red Fox, chief of the Blackfoot tribe. I am told that you have entered into Blackfoot territory and have things to trade us for safe passage through our land. If we find you have offerings of value, we will allow your safe passage. If you do not, you will not be allowed to continue."

Bart pondered what Red Fox meant by the phrase "not allowed to continue." He hoped that in the worst case they would be turned back and not given permission to cross Blackfoot land. Bull noticed the woman he had seen the previous evening standing off to the side looking at him again. She did not seem to be like the other Indian women. When he looked directly at her, she again turned her eyes away.

Bart and Bull were allowed to gather the packs from their horses and bring them to the camp site where Red Fox and the rest of the brave raiding party were gathered. The two of them began opening some of the packs and unloading items that they thought may have been interesting to the Indians. There were heavy cast iron pans and pots, eating utensils, metal plates, cups, kettles, knives, revolvers, scissors, clothing, boots, and mining equipment. The braves immediately went for the revolvers. Bart had tried to hide them but it was too late.

One of the braves picked up one of the revolvers and pointed it into the air and squeezed the trigger. When it went off, the other braves ran up and took the other two revolvers that Bart had partially hidden under a blanket. They were gone. Suddenly the whole group of Indians descended on the goods like a pack of wolves on a carcass. They began snatching up everything in sight.

Bull had a pack that he had yet to open, and the Indians did not seem to care about his pack. Bull slowly opened the pack and he picked up a hair brush. He looked at the woman who had starred at him. He held up the brush and pointed it at her. She looked to her left and then to her right to see if he was gesturing at someone else. No; he was motioning to her to come get the brush. She blushed. She did not move however. So Bull went over to her and handed her the brush.

There was a brave that had been busy pilfering Bart's belongings that now noticed what was happening. He immediately ran over to the woman and knocked the brush from her hand. He glared at Bull and said something to him in his native language. Bull was not one to back down to threats, so he bent down and picked up the brush and again handed it to the woman. This time the brave grabbed the brush and threw it into the nearby fire. Bull began to rear back to hit the brave and instantly the woman grabbed his arm and said,

"It would not be wise for you to strike the Chief's son."

Bull lost his anger immediately when he felt the woman's gentle touch. He felt a chill go through his body. He was amazed that she spoke to him in perfect English. He was stunned.

"You speak English." He stated.

"I am sorry, I cannot talk to you."

Indeed she should not have spoken to Bull, as the brave stepped between them and pointed for Bull to return to his pack. When Bull looked at the woman she would not return his gaze.

Bull returned and opened his own pack, no one approached, except the brave that he now knew was the Chief's son. The brave picked up the pack and again with a fury in his eyes, said something to Bull. He turned and walked away with Bull's entire pack. Bull started after him but this time Bart grabbed him by the shoulders.

"Bull, if you go after him they will kill you. Just let it go."
Bull did not like to let things go.

Red Fox had watched all that had happened. He walked over to Bull saying.

"That squaw is Running Deer. She is promised to my son as his wife. They are to be married the next full moon. My son, Grey Wolf, is a very jealous man. You would be wise not to challenge him."

Later that day the tribe had finished dividing up the spoils they had taken from the men's packs. They had cleaned out the entire gear that Bull and Bear had brought with them. Bull was furious. Not about his belongings. He was furious that his gift of the brush had been thrown into the fire---by Grey Wolf.

That night Bull was lying in his teepee. The guards were no longer posted outside as they had been the previous night. Bull could not sleep. He heard footsteps outside. He pulled his knife from its sheath, and crept over to the doorway. The flap of the door pushed in and Bull grabbed the intruder and pulled him inside. He was shocked when he saw that it was Running Deer; the woman promised to Grey Wolf.
Running Deer winced as she was roughly pulled into the tepee. She looked at Bull. Bull said.

"I am sorry; I thought that you may have been Grey Wolf."
She hurriedly spoke.

"I cannot stay long. If I am found in here we will both die. My name is really Abigail Thomas. I was taken from my parents when I was eight years old. I was captured by the Crow Indians and had lived with them for many years until a

Blackfoot raiding party took me two months ago. Be careful of Grey Wolf, he is a very violent and jealous man. Do not give him an excuse, or he will kill you."

"Why did you come to me if it is so dangerous?" Bull asked.

"I do not wish to be Grey Wolf's wife. You are the first white man I have seen in—" she stammered not completing the sentence.

"You want me to get you out of here?" Bull questioned.

"I---I don't know what I want from you." She answered. "I better leave now."

She left quickly, leaving Bull to wonder; what he could possibly do. In less than a minute, Bull heard a scream, and he knew who it was. He ran out of the teepee to see Running Deer on the ground about a hundred feet away. Grey Wolf was standing over her with a knife in his hand. Bull didn't think: he just charged at the Indian.

Grey Wolf was shocked when he turned and saw the giant running towards him. He was not accustomed to being challenged by anyone, let alone an unarmed white man. Grey Wolf was not a small man. Tribal members were all afraid of him, not only because he was the Chief's son, he was also a fearsome warrior. Before Bull got close to Grey Wolf there were five warriors that charged at Bull. They came directly at Bull who knocked four of them to the ground. By that time another five warriors joined the brawl. It took all ten of them to take Bull to the ground.

Grey Wolf had seen Running Deer come from Bull's teepee and his jealousy boiled like a volcano erupting. He had pushed her to the ground and surely would have killed her had Bull not interrupted him. However; it now appeared that there were two people that were destined to die. Bull and Running Deer.

The Chief sat down that evening with three of the tribal elders. They told the Chief that this dispute must be settled fairly. The Chief's son could not be shown favor, if he was to one day be a Chief himself. He had to win his battles on his own. That was the advice the elders gave to Red Fox.

The Chief took their advice in consideration and told them that he would have his decision the next day. Bull had been bound hand and foot, and was being well guarded. Bart was not allowed to talk with him.

The Chief reached his decision. The next morning he announced that Bull and Grey Wolf would have a contest to decide who would claim Running Deer. The contest would be that evening, and it would be a contest to the death. The Chief had no doubt that Grey Wolf would be able to be able to kill a weak-willed white man, even one as large as this one.

Chapter 12   Butte, Montana

The Chauncey Express, as Franklin called it, was seen coming in a cloud of dust from the south. It was the stagecoach from Pierre, South Dakota, returning to Mandan. We had been given mementos of our visit with the Lakota. I was given the necklace that Screaming Eagle had worn. It was the one that had bear claws strung with small turquoise stones in between each claw. Franklin was given a jacket made of elk hide. It was a beautiful jacket with colorful beadwork strung vertically on the chest, and fringe down each arm and at the waist. I was somewhat envious of the excellent jacket, until Screaming Eagle told me that my necklace would protect me from evil spirits. That made up for the jacket. Maybe!

Screaming Eagle brought us by horseback to the stagecoach road, and then told us;

"The stagecoach guard would probably shoot me if he saw me. He probably would think that I was going to scalp him."

We both laughed at this Indian's understanding of what most white men thought of them. We said our goodbyes, and thanked him for his sage advice and for the gifts. He raised his hand, palm outward and smiling said:

"How." Again a mockery of how Indians were thought to talk by white men. He had a good sense of humor.

Chauncey

We got on the stagecoach listening to disrespectful words from the driver who was the same one that warned us about the murderous redskins two days earlier. I thought it best not to say anything, since some people would always be confused with facts versus their opinions.

Upon arriving back in Mandan, we checked to see what time the train was scheduled to depart. The stationmaster reported that it would be leaving on the following morning. We checked back into the boardinghouse where we had left our baggage and spent the rest of the day talking to people in Mandan.

The Mandan area was infamous as the campsite of the Louis and Clark expedition that had stopped here the first winter of their journey almost ninety years ago. We heard many stories that had been passed on from the natives. One woman that we talked to claimed to be the daughter of Sacagawea's sister. She did not appear to me to be of Indian offspring, but she did have interesting stories to tell.

The next morning we were onboard the westbound train headed for new adventures. After we had travelled for three hours across flatland area we found the landscape change dramatically. There were no longer flat expanses of grassland, but miles and miles of precipitous barren hills of bluish-purple hue.

I could not imagine trying to find my way through these lands on foot or horseback. There were so many naked valleys and hills that lacked any trees or grasses. I wondered out loud to Franklin if we were actually entering the mountains of the west. A stranger across the aisle from us told us that this area was called the "Badlands." He said that

Teddy Roosevelt not only hunted around this land, he owned a ranch that I helped build.

He told us his name was Bill Sewall. He told us how Mr. Roosevelt hired him and friend Wilmot Dow as hunting guides in Maine. Later they had built the Elkhorn ranch here in the badlands and managed Roosevelt's large cattle herd for the last three years. Mr. Sewall told us he was headed back to the Elkhorn for the last time as the ranch was being closed down. Sewall had moved his family back east. The train stopped to load coal and water at a stop called Medora, and this is where Mr. Sewall bid us farewell.

Franklin and I went to the sleeper car after a supper that was supplied to us in the dining car. The sleeper was a contradictory name for a bed compartment. There were narrow bunks that were no more than twenty inches wide canvas hammock type beds with a scant sheet for covers. A partition of cloth curtain material could be pulled to give a measure of privacy. I got to sleep in the top bunk and had some trouble finding sleep with all of the clacking of the rails and chugging of the steam engine that could be very loud though; I was accustomed to the noisy snoring of my brother through many years. I was glad when sleep finally overcame the clamor.

It was early morning when I awoke having actually slept well since last checking my watch at midnight. What had awakened me was the train slowing down and coming to a halt. I climbed out of the bunk and actually stepped on Franklins arm while descending. Franklin let out a yelp and a cuss word being startled awake by someone stepping on him. I apologized for my clumsiness and told him;
	"The train is stopping, you might want to get up, and I

think Indians are attacking."
Franklin jumped from his bunk like being shot from a gun.
He was in his long johns and hurriedly pulled on his trousers
and boots. He ran over to a window, pulled the curtain and
saw a train station with our fellow passengers discharging
from their cars.

"You devil" He said in exasperation.
"Time to eat." I said.

We were in Custer, Montana along the Yellowstone River,
another place with rich historical significance. The battlefield
at Little Bighorn lay fifty miles to the south of us. Chief
Bigfoot had told us of the conflict that he had been in along
with Crazy Horse, Sitting Bull, and Chief Gall in their battle
with George Armstrong Custer. We would have loved to
travel down to see this site that Big Foot had told us about, but
our train would not be delayed this time. We stayed at Custer
for about two hours while the train was again refueled and a
new crew took over the train operation.

That day was one of the highlights of our trip that I will
never forget. After leaving Custer, we sat at the windows and
were amazed at the sights that would change with every mile.
We saw the snowcapped mountains as we travelled further
west. I had never imagined the immensity and majesty of
mountains. Our mouths dropped open in awe with each
curve in the tracks that brought us a new landscape. The
following day we arrived in Butte, Montana. This is one of the
places we would begin our search for information about Bart
and Bull. The first order of business was to find a place to
stay. This town is much bigger than we imagined.

The train station was on the south side of town. We asked
those around us where we could find a good place to stay for

a couple days. We were told "Good Luck" in finding anything! It was quickly apparent to us that this was a large and very dirty city. When I looked to the north there was a haze of smoke that hung in the air. What caused it I did not know? And, there were people everywhere. We stopped at six or seven hotels and boarding houses, I lost track after three. There were no available rooms at any of them, and, of course, we asked if anyone had heard of two men named Bart and Bull: that too was unsuccessful. Someone recommended that we go up to a place called Corktown, on the north side of town. A place there called the Mullin House was very large, and may have a room for us.

It was a mile or more across town and we continued to stop at hotels all through town without success. We were getting worried about finding anything at all. The Mullin House was a boarding house facility and only took people on a monthly basis. That was nice to find out now after a mile trek for nothing. Eventually we stopped at a saloon to get something to eat. There was a miner to whom we talked for a long time. He said that there had been a rush of miners that came to Butte when silver was found around ten years ago. Since then there has been a constant influx of miners for copper. He said copper is the gold of yesterday. Copper is in demand for what he called electrification. He offered to take us out to see some of the mining operations.

We followed him to the far northern edge of town. Everywhere there were tall piles of what he said were tailings from the mines. Smoke billowed from piles of copper ore being processed. Triangular shaped structures speckled the landscape like the teepees of the Indian reservation. We saw a stream that meandered through the mining area that looked like yellow-green urine. There was no vegetation growing either by the creek or anywhere around the naked piles of tailings. It had been poisoned by the water or the air, or both.

I thought once more about our visit with Screaming Eagle and how he reminded us of how things changed when the white man came to their land, and how they implored the Creator to return their lands to the way they had been in the past. I think I agreed with him. The land that I saw before me was no longer scenic or beautiful. It looked more like a scene that I would picture in Dante's inferno. It was in stark contrast to the beauty that Franklin and I had seen on our train trip through the landscapes coming out west.

Our miner friend also had a recommendation for a place to stay. He recommended a widow lady that lived in a house that had rooms for rent. He told us she would be glad to have a few dollars of extra income in exchange for a room in which to sleep. We asked our new friend if he knew of two characters by the name of Bart and Bull. He said that there were no miners here that he knew of by that name or by the physical description that we gave him.

We went to the woman's address that he had given us and found that it was a very nice house with lots of flowers planted in the yard and a well maintained exterior. The woman's name was Mrs. Patricia McMillan, and we soon were made aware of her entire life history. Not that we were annoyed at all by her soliloquy. She had a very interesting tale to tell. It was just that the tale took two hours to relate and I was rather worn out from the long journey and was ready for a decent night's sleep without the clackity- clack of the train track. Franklin on the other hand was all ears, and didn't seem the least bit tired. Oh, did I mention. She wasn't that old, maybe fifty--- and she had a young daughter that was twenty something. Her name was Maureen. Franklin's eyes lit up like a lantern. He took a shine to Maureen the minute we walked in the door. That was why he was so attentive. I excused myself and was shown to a room where there were two nice sized beds in comparison to the gunny sacks we had slept in for a week on the train. I was asleep the second my head hit the soft down pillow.

The next morning I saw Franklin sleeping in the bed across from me and wondered what time he had come to bed. When he finally awoke we decided to go get some breakfast at the café where Mrs. McMillan told us she worked. We followed the directions she had given us and came upon the café. It was called "McMillan's Café." A humble woman she was. She never told us she owned it. We went inside and found Maureen waiting on tables along with two other fine young women waitresses. There were easily thirty-five people in the room and most of them were miners heading to work or coming home from work. Mrs. McMillan was cooking in the kitchen. The aroma of coffee, bacon, flapjacks and potato pancakes was heavenly. Maureen saw us come in and seated us at one of her tables. I thought Franklin was going to trip over his own two feet as he followed her to the table. We ordered coffee and a stack of buckwheat cakes and bacon. It was good to have a real homestyle meal again. Franklin said.
"I think we should stay in this town a while."
"Whatever for?" I replied trying my best to get his goat.
I think this is a nice town and there are so many mines around here I'm sure we can find work. (Franklin was a very good carpenter.) Still being the devil's advocate, I said.
"I find the local landscape to be rather depressing compared to all the wondrous things we saw on the way out here. Maybe we should move on."

Chauncey

"Chauncey, this is the biggest town between San Francisco and Chicago. We need to spend some time here to make sure that the two B's (as he referred to Bart and Bull) are not here."

"Are you sure there isn't some other reason you want to stick around." I said.

Franklin could not suppress a smile.

"OK, now I know you're just givin me a hard time. She is nice, you know."

We ended up spending a lot of time in Butte, Montana.

Chapter 13   The Challenge

Bull was untied at sundown. He had been given no food or water since last evening when he was bound. Little did the Indians know that the more they did to humiliate and weaken Bull, the more resolute he became. They escorted Bull to an open area that was surrounded by braves all with fierce-looking face painting and dressed in full battle garb. Bull stood in the middle of the area and did not look around. He just stood and waited them out. It was a game they were playing with him.

He stood alone for at least a half-hour, but he didn't move. It was now almost completely dark out; the only light was from a fire. Finally he heard some chatter among the braves. Out of the crowd around him strode Grey Wolf. He was bare chested. He had red streaks radiating from the middle of his chest and black around his eyes. His forehead and cheeks were all white, and he had a necklace of bear teeth strung around his neck. When he reached the inside of the circle of braves he raised his arms and gave a war cry. All of the braves responded with cries of their own.

Bull was not impressed. He motioned toward Grey Wolf with a "come hither" gesture. That is when the odds changed.

One of the braves threw Grey Wolf a long hunting knife. It was one of the knives that they had taken from Bart's possessions. Grey Wolf smiled at Bull and advance toward him. This was not going to be a fair fight. Bull slowly circled to his right. Grey Wolf held the knife in his right hand, so Bull knew to stay on Grey Wolf's left side. When Grey Wolf got within four feet of Bull he started making short jabbing gestures with the knife. Not close enough to make contact but keeping Bull at slightly more than arms length.

Bull continued moving to his right. Grey Wolf had to keep turning to keep Bull in front of him. Bull was in a slightly crouched stance with both arms lifted to shoulder level from his side. Grey Wolf made a quick step forward while jabbing ahead with his knife. Bull took a quick step to the right. The knife whished through the air six inches from him. Grey Wolf next tried a move to incapacitate Bull by dropping low to attempt to cut Bull in the leg. Bull stepped back when he saw the move and smashed a sledge hammer blow to the top of Grey Wolf's head. Grey Wolf stumbled and almost fell, but jumped back up. A normal man would have been on the ground, but Grey Wolf now knew that he could not make any more mistakes with this man.

The circling continued. The braves were getting a little restless and began to chant and urge Grey Wolf to attack. Bull, sensing the hesitance of Grey Wolf, antagonized him by moving his fingers inward as if to say: "Come and get me." Grey Wolf was patient, however, and continued to look for an opening. This time Bull gestured again with his hands and said. "C'mon, chief, show me what you got." Grey Wolf understood some of the words and his anger rose. He lunged at Bull with a sweep of the knife going toward the left side of Bull's chest. This time instead of going to the right, Bull completely surprised Grey Wolf and did a complete pirouette to the left and swung a left hand down on the forearm of Grey Wolf. The knife flew from Grey Wolf's hand, landing five feet away. Neither man tried to pick it up which would have left them vulnerable.

Bull now had an advantage that he immediately utilized. He went in low on Grey Wolf and was able to partially sweep one of his legs out from under him. He swept upward on the leg sending Grey Wolf into an off balance tumble backwards. Grey Wolf rolled over backward jumping to his feet before Bull could advance. Someone in the group of braves tossed Grey Wolf another knife. This time however, Chief Red Fox yelled out to Grey Wolf and said something to him. Grey Wolf hesitated, but did not give up the knife. He charged at Bull and this time he spun, anticipating correctly that Bull would do the same. Bull had tried the same move as before and realized he had made a mistake. Grey Wolf slashed at him as he spun and caught Bull in the left side and back with the slicing cut. It was not a deep cut, but if was a long nasty gash.

This time as Bull stood in a crouch, Grey Wolf mocked the gesture with his hands that Bull had made before. He mimicked the words also.

"C'mon Chief," he said.
Bull smiled at him. Blood was running down his side. Bull said.

"Is that the best ya got? Maybe ya need more help from your squaw buddies."

Grey Wolf knew enough English to understand exactly what Bull had just said; or especially the squaw part. His temper again interfered with his judgment. He charged at

Bull, approaching his injured side. Bull went completely to the ground and swept with his legs, hitting Grey Wolf behind his knees. Grey Wolf went face first into the dirt. Bull was on top of him with lightning speed before Grey Wolf could jump up. Bull grasped Grey Wolf's wrist that held the knife. Grey Wolf struggled mightily but could not overcome the 300 pounds of muscle that was pinning him down. Bull pulled the wrist up and back until Grey Wolf yelped in pain, dropping the knife. Bull picked the knife up. He looked over at Chief Red Fox. He also saw Running Deer in the background watching over the top of the braves. He struck Grey Wolf in the side of the head with his fist, knocking him into a semi-conscious state.

Bull got up and threw the knife on the ground in front of Chief Red Fox. He turned and walked away from Grey Wolf toward where Running Deer stood. Grey Wolf saw Bull walking away. He also saw the first knife that he had dropped three feet from him. He grabbed the knife and leapt to his feet and charged toward Bull. When he was three feet from plunging the knife into Bulls back, two things happened. Bull had locked eyes with Running Deer who was smiling at him. He was unaware that Grey Wolf was coming at him until he saw the shocked look in Running Deer's eyes. That was too late. The second thing that happened was: Bull heard a gunshot.

The gun shot did not come from Bart, and it was not from one of the braves. It was from Chief Red Fox, the father of Grey Wolf. The shot hit Grey Wolf directly in the heart. Grey Wolf fell at the feet of Bull who had not even had time to turn around and face his attacker. Red Fox walked slowly over to Bull. He spoke in a low voice.

"You are an honorable man. You defeated Grey Wolf,

and you could have killed him. You chose not to kill him. My son dishonored me and my tribe by trying to kill the man who had just spared his life. Such a man can never be a Blackfoot chief. You and your friend can remain with our tribe until you are well enough to travel. You will not be harmed. Running Deer is free to do as she pleases."

Red Fox turned and walked away while he spoke something in Blackfoot to the braves. His words were:

"There will be no harm done to this man or his friend. He is now responsible for Running Deer as well."

Chapter 14   A New Lead

 F ranklin really liked Butte. I was truthfully ready to
leave Butte and the smoke filled skies and barren landscape.
But Franklin got a job building a house for our miner friend
and his family. They were going to pay him eight hundred
dollars to build a single story three bedroom home. So I
helped Franklin with the building which took us five weeks of
steady work. I actually felt good about the building
experience. Franklin is really an excellent builder. He had
done building back in Indiana for our brother when he added
on to our mother's home, and helped our sisters and their
husbands build their homes. Since we were helping out our
miner friend by building his house, he helped us by putting
out the word that we were hunting two men by the name of
Bart and Bull. There were no miners in the area that had any
knowledge of two such men.

Maureen and Franklin had become very good friends. She
brought us a noon meal at our building site every day. She
and Franklin would sit on lumber in the back of the house to
eat their lunch. I would try to give them some privacy and eat
on the front steps. When we were nearly finished with the
house, we were approached by another family to possibly
build a house for them. This was the point of decision for
both of us. Should we stay and become businessmen building
houses? Or should we continue the quest that we had started
in Indiana?

Franklin and I had a long discussion about the future. I knew very well, that he had strong feelings for Maureen and she for him. I did not wish to pull him away from a possible future with this woman. So, I told him that I would travel alone down to Virginia City, Montana and check out that area for our two criminals and then come back to him with a report on what I found. It was only a fifty mile trip down to Virginia City so I told Franklin I would be gone a week or two at the most.

I purchased a horse with some of the money we had made on the house building, and bought a load of supplies to give me shelter on the way. Maureen and her mother also packed me some food to take along. We all bid farewell, and I headed east through an area called Whiskey Gulch and then turned southeast until I reached the Jefferson River. I pitched my tent that night at a place called Twin Bridges where the Big Hole and Beaverhead Rivers join to form the Jefferson. I got directions from the locals and again headed to the southeast in search of the Ruby River and Alder Creek. After I traveled about fifteen miles I began to see many small shacks along the many rivers and creeks that I passed through. Soon there was a cluster of cabins along a small creek. I spoke to some men that were working at a sluicing operation and found out that this was Alder Creek. Virginia City was three miles away. I rode into town and it appeared to be a smaller version of Butte. There were lots of saloons and boarding houses. I got a room in a small place called the Placer Hotel.

I went to my room and freshened up and took a short nap before going out to seek some information. The first place I went to was a saloon. I went in and ordered a beer at the bar. The old timer bartender told me had been there for twenty years. I asked him:

"Do you happen to know two men that go by the name Bart and Bull?"

He looked at me astonishingly.

"Who wants to know?

"I do. They murdered my father." I said.

"Oh: well then yes I do remember them. They skedaddled out of here some fifteen years ago. You sure you want to get involved with those two? They're some pretty rough characters."

"I'm only trying to locate where they are at this time. I ain't looking to get in a shootout with them." I told him.

"Well, I ain't sure where they headed but they sure left here in a big hurry. Like I said; about fourteen, fifteen years ago."

"Do you know where they went?"

"Nope. But I know someone who might. Jim Amos. Owns the Nugget Saloon over on Wallace Street."

I thanked him and went directly to Wallace Street. My heart was pounding like it was Christmas morning and I was a little kid. I really couldn't believe that after all this time and all the distance I had travelled, I actually had found someone who knew these two. Then I began to have doubts. My old dreams resurfaced---the ones where Bart shoots me. Maybe these were common names---Bart and Bull. There were a lot of men named Bart. What were the chances that I had found the two I had been searching for in this immense land? I wasn't sure that I wanted to find out. What did I really want to do? I got to the Nugget and stood out in front for several minutes pondering what to do.

I went in.

"Could I talk to Mr. Amos, please? I asked the

bartender.

"Right over there." He said pointing at a corner table. He was drinking a beer and playing a game of solitaire.

"My name is Chauncey Miller. I am looking to find two men that you may know."

"Who would that be?" He mumbled, never looking up from his card game.

"Bart and Bull."

He immediately jerked his head up and looked at me like I had slapped him in the face. I felt him evaluating me as he slowly stroked his beard.

"You a lawman?"

"Nope, just a man looking for a needle in a haystack." I answered.

"Well, you found the right haystack but the needle is gone. Why you lookin for them?" He queried.

"Can you tell me their last names?" I asked not answering his question.

"Depends. He repeated. "Why you lookin?"
I wasn't sure if he was protecting them or if he was just curious.

"They murdered my father." I said, half expecting him to say he didn't know anything about them.

"Don't surprise me none. Those two ain't no friends-a-mine. Bart Decker and Bull Lukas. I think Bull's first name is Buster. But they ain't been around here for a long time. Left in a hurry, they did. I think the vigilantes were after them."

"You know where they went?" I queried.

"Bart told me they were heading up to Missoula, but I wasn't to tell no one. That's the last I saw either of them and the last I hope ta ever see them."

"I hear that was about fifteen years ago."

"Yup, that's about right, maybe fourteen."

"Did they know someone up there or you know why

they went there?" I inquired further.

"I don't know why they wanted to go there. Like I said, they were on the run. It was either stay here and get their necks stretched or leave."

He was unable to give me any further information or contacts that would have known more about them, so I bid him adieu, and thanked him for his help. He went back to his game of solitaire. I was happy to finally learn their last names; Bart Decker and Buster Bull Lukas. It would make things much easier for me in the future, trying to find their location. I don't know whether I am excited or scared.

Chapter 15   Abigail

Abigail Thomas (Running Deer) was a beautiful woman. She was tall with dark hair, parted in the middle with braids falling down below her shoulders. Her face was round with high cheekbones and amber colored eyes.   Bull thought she was the most strikingly beautiful woman he had ever seen. He was not sure if Abigail was interested in him as a way of escaping her captivity or if she was attracted to him. He wasn't sure he cared which reason she had as long as she wanted to go with him.

The first night after the battle with Grey Wolf, Bull found out the answer. Abigail came to his teepee, even though she still feared reprisal. She went up to Bull and kissed him full on the lips. Bull had not expected this and felt very awkward. No woman had ever kissed him before. In fact this was the first act of affection that he had felt since---never. Even his mother had treated him with disdain and ambivalence. The only men his mother had been interested in were men that would drink, cuss and have their way with her; which was to say, almost anybody that wore pants.

Bull was flooded with feelings in his soul he had never felt.

There was happiness, satisfaction, pleasure and excitement. All of which were unfamiliar to him. When Abigail stepped back and looked into Bull's eyes she saw a man that had been changed---in an instant. He wanted more of those feelings. Something that had been a void in his life was being filled. He felt whole, but he knew that he had more voids that needed filling, a lot more emptiness to satisfy. He now knew what he had been missing his entire life.

Abigail then told Bull.
"There is a brave that you need to watch closely. His name is Spotted Horse. He was Grey Wolf's closest friend. He has told his squaw that he will kill you before you can leave this camp. If you were not badly injured I would tell you to leave immediately, but you need to heal before you can travel. I will bring you medicine that will help your wound to heal, but your healing will be of no meaning if Spotted Horse has his way. Promise me you will not let him harm you."
Bull, tongue tied as he was, managed to say.
"No harm will come to me as long as you are helping me to heal."

The following days went slowly as Abigail tended to Bull's wound. The wound was almost ten inches in length and had been crudely stitched together by Abigail. Abigail's mom was a seamstress and had taught her to sew at an early age. Still, stitching up a large wound was not something to which she was accustomed. After a week, Bull was still unable to lift his arm up higher than his shoulder without great pain. Riding a horse was not an option for him at this time.

Spotted Horse's threat was very much on Abigail's mind. She had spent enough time with the Indians to know that they never made empty threats. They always said what they meant, and meant what they said. She was a good friend of Spotted Horse's squaw whose name was Peta. She talked to Peta more frequently since the fight between Bull and Grey Wolf. Peta told Abigail that Spotted Horse was not talking much to her anymore. His loss of his friend had brought him much sorrow and hatred. She was sure that Spotted Horse was going to do something soon. Abigail asked her.

"Is he not aware that Red Fox told the tribe that no harm was to come to the white man and his friend?"

"Spotted Horse thinks that Red Fox is a weak leader. He thinks that achieving revenge on your white brothers will raise his importance in the tribe. He desires to become Chief. The killing of this white man will ensure that his leadership will be sought after. Red Fox wants peace with the white man. Spotted Horse wants war. He wants to push the white men from our lands and make us once again a proud and unyielding people that will be feared. He knows your man is not yet strong because of his wound. He will strike soon." Peta told her.

"Will you tell me when Spotted Horse is going to attack?"

"I wish no harm to your white man, but I will not forsake my man."

"I understand. Abigail replied.
Abigail went to Bull and told him of her conversation with Peta.

"She tells me he will soon try to kill you. Are you able to ride?"
Bull chuckled.

"I am not able to ride, and would not leave if I could."
Abigail took hold of Bull and kissed him tenderly.

"I do not wish for you to be killed. I have been thinking about what it would be like to live among my own people again. What it would be like to start a life with you. If something would happen to you my life would again become futile."

Bull felt a tugging in his heart. He was willing to give his life for this woman. He told her so.

Bart could sense the changes that had come about in Bull. He could perceive that Bull was becoming more distant from him. He also knew that there was a developing relationship between Bull and Abigail. This caused insecurity in Bart that was escalating daily. Bart was a tall man, but not muscular. He was not a physically strong person. Bull had been his protector and bodyguard for the greater part of his life. No one could challenge Bart without confronting Bull. They were Siamese twins that were in the process of being separated.

It was a, dark, starless night that had an ominous stillness about it. It was a stillness that preceded a catastrophe. Bull was alone in his teepee and had been sleeping for several hours. Spotted Horse was wide awake and on the move. He carried with him the necklace of Grey Wolf. Revenge would soon be his. His leadership in the tribe would soon be acknowledged and Red Fox would have to recognize him as the new leader of the Blackfoot. He moved through the darkness like a ghost through a graveyard---silently, quietly. He neared the teepee in which Bull was slumbering. An owl hooted. Spotted Horse stopped. The owl was an omen. It meant that the wise spirit was watching him and did not approve. But bad omens were not enough to stop Spotted Horse. He took out his knife to cut his way into the teepee.

Four braves had also been ghosts in the darkness. The braves converged on Spotted Horse as he took out his knife. Red Fox was the fifth person to come out of the shadows. He spoke to Spotted Horse who was now being detained by the four braves.

"Did you think Red Fox was stupid? I stated that no one was to hurt this white man. You have disobeyed me and have humiliated yourself."

Bull was awakened by the commotion and came out of the teepee. He listened as he heard what Red Fox was saying.

"Spotted Horse is no longer a Blackfoot. He has shamed me and our tribe. His name will not be spoken by the Blackfoot again. He will be sent away, never to return to the lands of the Blackfoot. Take him, naked to the mountains and release him there."

Red Fox turned and walked away. Spotted Horse was removed from the tribe, never to return to the Blackfoot.

Chapter 16   Missoula

I stayed in Virginia City for two more days. I inquired among people in town for further information concerning Bart Decker and Buster Lukas. There was a lot of information about the bad things that Bart and his accomplice had foisted upon the locals. No one other than Jim Amos could tell me where they had gone. I was anxious to get back to my brother and tell him what I had learned. I mounted my horse and headed back to Butte. I felt good after all this time I had a firm lead on the two that had caused my family so much pain.

I got to the McMillan house late evening of the next day. Mrs. McMillan was knitting in the living room when I came into the house. Franklin and Maureen were sitting on the couch together opposite of Patricia. When I came in, they were all smiles. I looked at them and said.

"What? You all look like a cat that swallowed a canary."

Patricia looked to her daughter. Maureen looked at Franklin. Franklin grinned even wider.

I repeated.

"What's going on."

Finally Franklin said.

"Well, we wanted to tell you that Maureen and I are

planning on getting married."
I really wasn't surprised, but didn't expect this so soon.
I said.

"Congratulations to both of you. I am pleased
that you found someone that would put up with you
Franklin."

"Gee thanks, brother."

"When is the happy day going to be?" I queried.

"We haven't decided on that yet. Maybe this fall. What
did you find out in Virginia City?"
I explained to them all that I had discovered during my trip
and that Missoula would be my next destination.

"Funny thing about that." Franklin said. "Mrs.
McMillan and Maureen have been talking about moving
away from Butte because of all the mining and smelting
concerns. Missoula is one of the places where they are
interested in relocating."
We talked for a while about places where it would be good for
them to live. I told them that Helena or Missoula would be
good places to establish a new McMillan's Eatery.

The following days we agreed the best option was for the
McMillan and Miller families moving to Missoula. We
discussed how we should find some property in Missoula on
which to build a house or a café. It was decided that Franklin
and I would travel up to Missoula and look over the
availability of housing and potential buildings for a café.
Maureen and her mother would not join us until their current
house and café were sold. Mrs. McMillan authorized Franklin
to negotiate on her behalf in purchasing a new building.
Franklin really must have made a good impression on both of
the McMillan's.

In mid-summer my brother and I departed from Butte and

were on the move again. This time we travelled by horseback instead of train. Not nearly as comfortable on the rear end. I think we both had butt blisters after several days. From Butte we followed Silver Bow Creek to Deer Lodge. There is where we began following the Hell Gate River that some called the Clark Fork River, which led us all the way to Missoula. It took us three days of travel to get to our destination. Missoula was not as large a town as Butte but it is a lot more beautiful with the Blackfoot and Bitterroot Rivers joining the Clark Fork twisting its way through town. There were the snow capped Bitterroot Mountains to the west of the large expanse of the Missoula valley lying before us.

We easily found a room in a hotel and boarded our horses at the livery nearby. We were both tired and sore from the long ride, so we turned in for the night. The following morning we had breakfast in the dining room of the hotel. Mediocre food at best compared to McMillan's Café. Based on this, the McMillan's had a great opportunity to establish a good eatery that could surpass the local cuisine. After breakfast we walked the downtown area looking for both location and availability of buildings that were for sale.

After we eliminated several places, we found one that had potential. It was a corner hardware store that the owner was selling because he and his family were moving to Oregon. Franklin and I discussed between us about this being the perfect location for a restaurant. If we placed windows on the side of the building it would have a panoramic view of the river while the front windows had a view of the mountains to the west. It was in our opinion, an ideal spot. The closest restaurant was three blocks away and we would be in the middle of a busy commercial area. Now we needed to negotiate a good selling price.

We went in to the hardware store with a strategy. We did not want to run a hardware store so that was to be our negotiation tactic. The owner wanted three thousand dollars for the building with the entire hardware inventory. We asked him what he planned on doing in Oregon. He was planning on staying with what he knew, and that was to start another hardware store.

Franklin told him that buying new inventory in Oregon would probably be costly because hardware would need to be shipped all the way from St. Louis. High freight costs, Franklin told him.
"You have already paid the freight costs for your current stock. Why would you pay for shipping all the way from St. Louis when you could just ship it from here to Oregon?"
The owner thought that Franklin had a good point, and said.
"Won't you gentlemen have to pay for shipping to restock all my goods?"
We looked at one another.
"We plan on bringing in our stock from Butte, so that will not be a problem for us."
The owner told us that the building needed some work on the roof and some of the rest of it needed fixing up, so he would sell us the building by itself for four hundred dollars.
Franklin and I almost fell over. We were expecting him to ask for at least a thousand dollars for it so we both said at the same time.
"We'll take it."
Franklin was so excited I thought he would wet his pants.
"I wish I could tell Maureen and Mrs. McMillan about this right away. They would be so happy with this location and especially with the price. I need to send them a telegram right away. I can have this place all fixed up in a month at

most. The roof just needs a few shake shingles replaced and by the time we put new windows in the south wall we only have to add a kitchen area in the back to make it completely ready for them. "

I said,

"Whoa, slow down brother. We still have to purchase stoves, tables, chairs and find out how the McMillan's want us to decorate the interior."

Franklin was like a race horse standing at the starting line chomping at the bit to run the race. He was already rounding the first curve before the race started.

We closed the deal the following day and at week's end, we were the proud owners of an empty building. Even I was excited.

Chapter 17   Mended Wounds

The road to recovery for Bull was longer than he

expected. Being unable to raise his arm was not conducive to riding a horse. Abigail tended to Bull every day. She applied herbs given to her by the medicine man. They were to prevent the wound from becoming infected.   The Blackfoot had begun to accept Bull since Spotted Horse had been cast out of tribe. They had even given him an Indian name. It was Angry Bear. They said that he fought like a wounded bear after Spotted Horse had cut him.

Bart, on the other hand, was not well received by the Blackfoot. He did not interact with any of the Blackfoot people. He rarely talked to Bull, and mostly stayed in his teepee. Bull did not make an attempt to deal with Bart's moodiness, he ignored it. Bart was almost contemptuous of not only Bull, but of Abigail. This did not sit well with Bull. He attempted to bring it up to Bart one day.

"Bart, why do you not speak with Abigail? She tells me you will not even say hello to her?"

"Because she is a dirty redskin." Was Bart's reply. Bull nearly hit him, and that was the last time they had spoken to one another.

It was now early spring and all of the mountain passes were blocked by snow, so Bull and Abigail were unable to leave until a warm-up occurred. When the rivers were running they would take their leave of the Blackfoot camp. It had been a hard winter but Bull was now healed and even had shown his prowess as a hunter. He helped the tribe's hunters to harvest some elk in the lower meadows near the Bitterroot River. During the winter, Abigail had sewn a striking long coat of elk skin for Bull. It fit perfectly. Not many store bought clothes fit Bull because of his large size.

Bull announced to Red Fox that he and Abigail would be leaving before the full moon when the spring melt had begun. Red Fox wished them well and gave them all of the packs of items that Bull had brought with him when he had been captured. Abigail presented Red Fox with an elk skin vest that she had sewed for him, with much colorful beading on the breast. Red Fox was very impressed and appreciative of the gift. Bull was given five horses to take with him. One week before the full moon, Abigail and Bull loaded their horses and prepared to leave. They were loading the horses when Bart came from his teepee.

"Are we leaving?" He asked.

"Angry Bear and Running Deer are leaving. You wouldn't want to travel with 'dirty redskins' would you?" Bull sneered.

"Bull you know I didn't mean anything by that. I have been stuck here by myself for three months with no one to talk to. I was just feeling sorry for myself. We need to travel together to make sure we don't get lost or attack by---uh---hostiles."

Bull gave him a derisive laugh.

"You can follow us if you like, but mark my word Bart. If you do not treat Abigail with respect and speak to her when spoken to, I will shoot you."

Bart followed Bull who rode side by side with Abigail. They followed the river called the Bitterroot for many days. They had to detour many miles in places to find suitable passage through streams swollen with the spring melt. On the fourth day of their travels, they approached a small hill to the north. Abigail saw them first.

"Bull, over there." She said pointing to the crest of the hill.

There were five Indians on horseback watching their approach. As they got closer, eight or ten more Indians appeared to the right and ten more on the left. Abigail recognized them as a Crow raiding party.
She said.

"I can talk to them. They will understand me. Do not act afraid or show them weakness."
Abigail proceeded to ride up to the leader of the Crow. She spoke to them in perfect Crow language. She told them she had lived among the Crow for many years with the leader "Fights with Fire." The Crow braves were impressed since they had heard many stories about Fights with Fire who was infamous for his many conquests.

Bull watched from a few horse lengths behind. Bart began getting nervous as some of the braves that surrounded them were talking and making what he perceived as threatening gestures toward him. Bart suddenly bolted, heading toward the braves that encircled them. Abigail turned and yelled something in Crow to the braves and they did not try to stop Bart they parted like the Red Sea to let him pass between them. Bart rode hard for about a half mile before he realized that no one was pursuing him. He stopped his horse and turned to look back. The Indians were leaving. Bull and Abigail were riding toward him. When they reached him he spoke to Abigail.

    "What did you say to those Indians that made them let me pass through?"

    "I told them that you were crazy in the head and possessed by an evil spirit. Most of us Indians are fearful of spirits that can pass into us from one that is evil."
Bart thought about that one for a while, but said nothing in response.
Bull said.

    "A thank you would be a proper response."
Bart looked at Abigail then at Bull.

    "Thanks." Was all he said.

After several days they approached the Missoula valley. Bart was pleased that he finally would be among white folks again. Abigail was apprehensive about being back in civilization for the first time in nearly twenty years. She looked more like an Indian woman than white, especially since she was dressed in moccasins, and animal skin clothes, had darkly tanned skin and long black pigtails. The first hotel that they stopped at in the town of Missoula would not let Bull and Abigail get a room. Bull became angry and would have caused a scene had Abigail not pulled him from the building.

Abigail had Bull go into a general store and buy her a dress, shoes and a hat. Abigail unbraided her black hair, put on the dress, shoes and hat. She looked so much different that Bull would not have recognized her had she walked by him on the street. They then went to another hotel and were able to get a room. Bart got a separate room in the same hotel.

Bull said to Abigail.

    "I don't know the proper way to do things, but how

about you and I get married?"

"Right now?" She asked.

"Yeah, why not right now?"

They went to a local justice of the peace and got married that evening. They were now Buster and Abigail Lukas. No more Angry Bear and Running Deer.

Bart Decker went to Bull's room the following morning and learned that Buster had gotten married to Abigail. He asked Bull if he wanted to accompany him to the Coeur D'Alene region of Idaho since rumor had it that many miners were having success finding silver there. Bull declined.

"My life is here with Abigail now. We plan on staying in Missoula for a long time. You go ahead to Idaho or wherever. Don't plan on me ever joining up with you again."

With that being said, Bart Decker and Buster Bull Lukas went their separate ways.

Chapter 18   The Hellgate

It was the fall of the year before Patricia McMillan and her daughter Maureen joined us in Missoula. Mrs. McMillan sold their house and Café in Butte. Franklin and I took two wagons down to Butte and moved all of their belongings up to Missoula. There was so much to move that we ended up buying a third horse and wagon in Butte in order to transport everything. Maureen drove the third wagon all the way to their new home.

Franklin and I had not only remodeled the old hardware store into a very luxuriant and picturesque restaurant; we had found a nice house for Mrs. McMillan. It also had room enough for Franklin and Maureen to live in until they were able to find a separate place of their own. I, on the other hand, had a room that I could live in on the second floor of the restaurant that was rather cramped, but adequate. We had fixed that up for me to live in until I also decided to move on to a new place. The restaurant was already drawing a lot of interest from the locals, since Franklin and I spent a lot of time working there and talking to passersby who would ask us what we were building.

The restaurant, Mrs. McMillan decided, would be called the "Hellgate Steakhouse". This name was in honor of the first settlement in Missoula. It was going to be the best steakhouse west of the Mississippi she said. When Patricia and Maureen saw it for the first time they were in awe of the work we had done. We had added the large picture windows in the west wall with a view of the mountains. We replaced the old windows that faced the river to the south with two large picture windows on either side of a heavy double door of rough sawn cedar with shiny brass door handles. The walls were all knotty pine with decorations of Indian headdresses, bows and arrows, old rifles, powder horns, wagon wheels, old crosscut saws, lumberjack tools, axes and so on. The tables were all natural wood with matching chairs made of knotty pine branches. Patricia McMillan ran over and gave us both a big hug. She said.

"This is the most beautiful place that I could imagine. I never dreamed it would be this nice in my most fanciful dreams. You two have done an outstanding job. I just hope that I can make my food worthy of the surroundings."
I replied.

"I have tasted your food and believe me when I say; your food will surpass any of the work that we have done here."

Patricia and Maureen worked on hiring staff to help in the kitchen and to wait tables. They figured to open the restaurant in three weeks. Franklin and I made signs and had some pamphlets printed up that advertised the grand opening of the "Hellgate Steakhouse". We distributed the pamphlets to local businesses and posted the signs around town. In the meantime the McMillan women were busy at work devising a menu and training staff for the opening.

The opening was a resounding success. The restaurant was packed the first day. Seating inside could accommodate about fifty people and people ended up being lined up outside for an entire block the entire day. People raved about the food and décor. Word spread around the area of the new restaurant in town. Patricia and Maureen were very pleased with their accomplishments. Franklin became famous for his building skills, and people sought him out to build for them. Franklin became as busy building as the McMillan's were in their restaurant. I helped out Franklin with his burgeoning building business and we soon had to hire additional men to assist. By the late fall of the year Franklin had fifteen men working for him. I knew that it was time for me to either decide to stay here and put down roots in this beautiful area or move on. I had mixed feelings both ways. The burning need to track down our father's killer had reduced itself to a little glowing ember.

Maureen and her mother went into a dress store in Missoula in search of a wedding dress. The store's owner greeted them. She said.

"Welcome, my name is Abigail Lukas. Can I help you find something?"
The name seemed kind of familiar to Maureen but she could not figure out where she had heard it before. Maureen told her that she was looking for a wedding dress. Abigail Lukas was a very friendly woman and they were shown several styles of dresses. Maureen found one dress in particular that she really liked. She purchased the dress and did a fitting for alterations. They then returned home. When she got home she was telling Franklin that she had purchased a wedding dress and that he would really like it. Then she told him.

"There was something about the woman at the store that I think was important but I can't quite put my finger on why."

They talked a while longer about the wedding coming up and then Maureen said.

"It was 'LUKAS'. That was her name. Abigail Lukas. Isn't that the name of the man you and Chauncey are looking for?"

"It is." Franklin replied.

"Maybe she is related somehow?"

Franklin didn't think that was a real possibility but he would tell Chauncey about it. Later that evening Franklin told me about it and we speculated on the chances that this woman, Abigail Lukas, was related to the man that we were seeking. I decided the next day Franklin and I would go to this store and talk to the woman named Lukas.

We walked into the store and immediately saw the tall dark haired woman that Maureen had described. She was talking to a customer so we wandered around the shop looking at the selection of goods. After a few minutes the woman came up to us and asked if she could help us. I said.

"I was wondering if you have had this store long?"

She answered.

"I started a seamstress business when my husband and I first move here nearly fifteen years ago. I got so much business that I started making clothes myself and then had to hire others to help me sew. We opened this store and as you can see we have a variety of clothes for all types of workers and all styles of women's clothes."

"You said you and your husband moved here fifteen years ago. Did you happen to come here from Virginia City?"

"Well no. I didn't come from there, but my husband, Buster, did."

Franklin and I looked at one another with a look of disbelief.

"Buster? Do folks call your husband Bull?"

"Why yes, he did used to go by Bull, but now he goes by Buster. Why, do you know him?"

"Uh, no, we don't exactly know him, but we had a mutual acquaintance in Virginia City."

I bought some bib overalls that seemed to be very well made and Franklin bought two pairs for himself. We left the store in a state of shock. We had found him. Now what? I told Franklin to head back home, I was going to see where they lived. Franklin took my purchase and I went across the street and waited for the store to close. Mrs. Lukas locked up the store at 5:00 pm and I followed her from two blocks back. She walked several blocks to a nice house. It was on a street that had many pleasant houses. I waited for an hour after Mrs. Lukas went in the house. I saw him coming from the opposite direction. There was no doubt. He was a huge man. He was at least six foot six or more and maybe three hundred fifty pounds. Bull Lukas. I felt sweat breaking out on my forehead. Who could ever face this giant without being scared to death? This was the man that was involved in my father's murder. I couldn't stay. I turned and walked the other direction.

I went back to the McMillan home. Franklin came out of the house when I got there.

"Did you find out if that was the Lukas we were looking for?"

"There is not a question about it. This is the same guy Franklin. I saw him. It is the 'Bull' we have been searching for. The guy is a mountain of a man."
Franklin stood with his mouth agape.

"What do we do now, Chauncey? It's not like you and I are going to go and challenge this guy."
I looked at Franklin.

"I never wanted this to be about revenge, Franklin. I first wanted to find the two men. So far we have found one of them. Remember, this Bull is not the one that killed our father. He was there, but according to Barbara, he is not the one that beat him to death. Let's think about this for a day and decide what to do."

We decided that I would go to the house and talk to Buster Lukas. I would either get the snot beat out of me or I would find out where Bart Decker was living. I was a little nervous about this but the following day was a Saturday so I went to the Lukas house and knocked on the door. A young girl around ten or eleven years old answered the door. I told her I was here to see Mr. Lukas. She was very polite and told me her name was Charlene, and asked me to come in. She had me sit in the living room and said she would get her father. I hadn't considered that this man could have a family. I always thought of him as a ruthless, heartless killer. The pictures in my mind of this man were changing as I sat waiting for him.

Buster 'Bull' Lukas walked into the room. He filled the doorway. I stood up to meet him. I said. "Mr. Lukas, my name is Chauncey Miller. I am from Goshen, Indiana."
Bull stood in the doorway and stared at me.
      "Goshen, Indiana? I do remember that place. Are you a lawman, coming to arrest me?"
Instead of being confrontational, I found Bull to be rather contrite.
      "No Bull, I am not a lawman. My father was the man that your friend Bart Decker killed with a shovel."
Bull walked over to a chair opposite me and sat down and put his head in his hands.
      "I knew my past would catch up with me. My running with Bart was going to come back on me sooner or later. I

knew I did wrong, staying with Bart all of those years. He is a bad man. I take the responsibility for what we done. I've tried to change my life, but knew that someday I would have to pay for my sins. I am sorry Mr. Miller for what we done to your father."

Bull continued shaking his head in his hands. I didn't say anything.

"If you want me to come back to Indiana with you for a trial, I will."

I experienced a sickening feeling in my stomach. This man with a beautiful young daughter and wife was willing to leave them and go back to Indiana for a trial. I didn't understand. I finally broke my silence.

"Bull, I have spent the past two years looking for Bart and Bull. My sister, Barbara, told me the story of what happened on that dreadful day when she saw Bart kill our father. I didn't know what I would do when I found them. Now I know."

He looked at me with unbelievable sadness in his eyes. He was resigned to the fact that I wanted to have him go back to Indiana with me. I said to him.

"I don't want you to go back with me."

"What? He said.

I told him that I did not hold him responsible for my father's murder. I did say however.

"I grew up without a father in my life. I do think that you could have stopped it from happening if you wanted to. You must have been very young since it was well over twenty years ago. I am not going to take you away from your family, since I know what it is like to grow up without a father. I ask that you be the best father that you can to your daughter and only one more thing. I want to know where Bart Decker is

living."
The sadness lifted from Bull's eyes.

"Bart Decker left here ten years ago headed to the Coeur D'Alene mining district of Idaho. We did not part on the best of terms. He hasn't contacted me since he left. I need to tell you what happened that day in Indiana.

When I knocked that man down---uh your father. I lost my balance and fell also. I had thought he was going to hit Bart with his shovel so I tried to stop him. When I turned and got off the ground, Bart was already hitting him with the shovel. That is when that girl screamed."

"That was my sister Barbara."

"When Barbara screamed, Bart yelled at me to go get her and don't let her get away. Bart was not one to leave witnesses behind, so I knew what he wanted me to do. When I ran after her, I decided right then that I was not going to hurt a little girl. So when I got to the ditch where she had been, I pretended to slip and fall into the mud. That gave her a good head start into some woods. So I got up and ran into the woods far enough that Bart couldn't see me and I stopped. I heard her still running in the distance. I waited a while and then started calling to Bart that I was lost and couldn't find my way out. He always thought I was stupid. Anyway, I had no intent on hurting your sister. I felt terrible about what Bart did to your father."

Abigail Lukas came into the room and said to Bull.

"Buster, are you OK? You are as pale as a ghost. Oh, you are the man from the store yesterday that knew Bull from Virginia City."

"Yes, we do have a common acquaintance, like I said. We were just talking about some things that happened to us a long time back."

Bull asked Abigail to get us something to drink. She left to go into the kitchen.

"Mr. Miller, I owe you for not taking me back to Indiana. I and my family are grateful to you. I have two boys besides my daughter, and they are grateful to you also. We run a sawmill here in town, if you need anything, you just let me know and it is yours."

Abigail brought two glasses of water in for us. I told them that my brother, Franklin was a builder here in Missoula and his future wife and mother-in-law had just opened the Hellgate Steakhouse.

"We've heard all about that place." They replied in unison.

"Good things are being said about that place, at the mill." Bull responded.

"You'll have to take me there, Bull." Abigail remarked.

"When you come, you tell the owner that Chauncey says your meal is on him."

Bull and I walked to the door, and we shook hands. Bull's hand engulfed mine like my hand was a child's. He told me again how grateful he was to me and reiterated that if I or my brother needed and help with the building business, that we should come to his mill and he would see that we got lumber at a large discount.

I walked to Franklin's home and proceeded to tell him what I had found out at the Lukas home. I told him Bull Lukas was not a bad man. He was young and happened to run with the wrong man. He is not the man we thought he was. He is grateful to us for not seeking to prosecute him.

That week Franklin and I read some bad news in the newspaper. Chief Big Foot that we had met at the Standing

Rock Indian Reservation in North Dakota, who had given us such sage advice, had been killed. He was killed in a massacre at a place called "Wounded Knee" in South Dakota, along with one hundred and fifty or more men, women and children. I would never forget the kindness and insight that this man had given to us when we visited his home.

Franklin and Maureen were married early that winter. I explained that my search was only half done; I was planning on heading to Idaho in the spring. Ten weeks after the wedding I packed up my things. I purchased a pack mule along with my horse and loaded them up with my belongings. I was on my way to Idaho. The Mullan road leads west out of Missoula and leads the way into Idaho's mining areas. I would travel this road on my destination to the Coeur D'Alene mining district.

Chapter 19   The Split

Bart Decker left Missoula in a bad mood. He did not think that Bull was being fair with him; after all he had done for Bull. Bull just did not appreciate it. Bart rode out of the Missoula valley headed west and north. This is the first time that Bart had been on his own, since — since never. He had always had someone to rely on. Now he had no one to watch his back, or his front for that matter. The first night he spent in the foothills of the Bitterroot Mountains he nearly had a panic attack when he listened to all the night noises. He heard things that had never bothered him before. Hoots, howling, twigs cracking, and he even thought he heard voices. Bart got little sleep during the night.

When he finally did go to sleep he dreamt that the Blackfoot had captured him again and were going to burn him at the stake. He awoke and found he had rolled too close to his fire. He was elated to see the dawn of light in the east that morning. He decided to keep riding that day until he got to a town. No more nights alone in the forest. There was a trail he followed that led into Idaho and he stayed on this trail until well after dark that night. He was more afraid of camping again in the woods than falling down an embankment on the trail. Around midnight he saw some buildings in what looked to be a small town. Once he got into the town, which was little more than a handful of buildings, he could not find any place that had lights in their windows. He unpacked his bedroll, tied up his horse, and lay down and went to sleep behind one of the houses.

The following morning, Bart again woke up early with the crack of dawn. He heard someone talking down the street. He walked toward the talking. There was a man and woman standing outside a house talking. Bart said.

"Top of the morning to you."

They looked him up and down and said.

"You the man that was sleeping outside the Walkers place last night?"

Bart wondered why they seemed concerned, so he replied.

"My horse got spooked last night on the trail several miles east of here. He threw me off and just took off running down the road. I walked for two or three hours before I caught up with him. I saw the houses down here and didn't want to wake no one at that hour, so I just slept on the ground til this morning. By the way, what is the name of this place?"

"This is Mullan, Idaho. What's your name, mister? They queried.

Bart hesitated. He was well known in Virginia City, and the law may even have been looking for him. Miners were coming to this area from western Montana all the time. Some of them may have known the name Bart Decker. So Bart made a quick decision.

"My name is Carl Dunston." He lied.

"Where are you headed, Mr. Dunston?"

Again, Bart was indecisive.

"I'm headed to the next good sized town."

"Oh, well then you're headed to either Wallace or Kellogg."

Bart didn't know either name so he picked one.

"Yeah, I'm headed to Wallace."

"Well you ain't got far to go caus Wallace is only eight miles west a here."
Bart, or whatever he was calling himself now, told them he would be headed out. He got on his horse and rode off toward Wallace, Idaho.

When Bart rode into Wallace down the main street he saw a young woman in front of a building.
She waved at Bart and gave him a big smile.
"Do you need a place to stay? We have rooms available." She crooned.
Bart was a sucker for a pretty face and immediately told her he needed a room for the night.
"It's twenty-five dollars a night." She stated.
"What! Twenty-five dollars. Are you crazy?" Bart bellowed.
"That's the going rate honey. You must be new in town.
"I might be new in town but I ain't stupid. I'll find my own place to stay."

Bart stopped at the only other "hotel" but found that they charged the same price. Bart ended up sleeping outside of town in a small area along a creek. His horror of spending twenty-five dollars a night outweighed his fear of staying outside in the woods at least for one more night. During the night, he once again found that he got little sleep; but he got a brilliant idea. He had some gold that he had kept from the Blackfoot Indians when he was captive. In the morning, he would go to the bank or assay office and cash in his gold.

The next morning he found an assay office. They told him his gold was worth around a thousand dollars. Bart exchanged his gold for the cash. Then he went out looking for

a building to buy. This turned out to be a more difficult task. He could not find a vacant building available. He did find a room in a small boarding house though, for the sum of fifteen dollars a week. The old man that owned the house told Bart that the only places to stay in town were bordellos, and all were owned by the same man. He charged the same exorbitant amounts at his places of business.
Bart asked him.

"Who is this guy that owns everything in town?

"His name is Jack Warden." The old man told him.

"He ain't someone you want to mess with."

"What is the name of the meanest toughest sob in this area that isn't connected to this man named Warden? " Bart inquired.

"I guess that would be Leif Peterson. He is a lumberjack and bear trapper that is working up north of town on nine-mile road. You would be wise not to upset that man either or you will have a short stay in Wallace."

Bart asked around town until he found the location where Leif Peterson was staying. That evening Bart travelled to Leif's place. Bart knocked on the door. A large red haired man with a big red mustache answered the door.

"Who are you and whaddaya want?" Leif said roughly.

"My name is Carl Dunston." Bart replied. He would have to remember the new name he was using.

"I am going to make you a rich man." Carl said.
Leif scoffed.

"Yah, sure." Is all he said
Carl went on anyway.

"One man named Warden owns the only two places to get a room in Wallace. I hear that he pretty much runs the whole town. There are miners coming here in droves to check out the area and unless they want to pay twenty five bucks a pop for one night, they have nowhere else to stay. I plan on starting up my own place and will charge only ten bucks a night. Now which place would you stay in if you came to Wallace?

Leif looked at him in disbelief.

"Whaddaya think I can do to help run a hotel; are you nuts? I cut down trees and trap bear."

"Look, Mr. Peterson: I ain't lookin to turn you into a business man. I need some muscle to help me if I am going to challenge the man that runs everything in town. You can get some of your buddies to help out, I'll leave that part up to you. How much money do you make a week cuttin trees?

"I clear fifteen to twenty in a good week." Leif responded.

"I'll give you fifty a week to start out. Once we get a place up and running I'll split all of our income with you 60/40. Figure this out. If we have fifteen rooms at ten bucks a night: that calculates to be a thousand and fifty bucks a week. That is four hundred and twenty dollars in just a week that would be all yours. All you would have to do is keep our place safe. If we bring girls in and charge another ten bucks a night, that doubles what we could make, and it's still less cost than the other places are charging.

Carl could see the light come on in Leif's eyes. That was three times the money he could bring in working almost twenty days. Leif thought it over for about two seconds.

"You got a deal, Mister. What did you say your name was?"

Carl smiled.

"Carl Dunston: partner! How bout you and I go lookin for a building to start our business?"

Chapter 20   The Homestead

I am on my own for the first time ever. With nine brothers and sisters, believe me when I say, I was never alone. Maybe in the outhouse I could find a little solitude, for a bit. But inevitably, one of my sisters would come banging on the door. "Chauncey, Chauncey, hurry up. I have to go bad". That was my little piece of privacy. Now that I reflect back, it wasn't all that bad to have family around all the time. I never wanted for a good conversation or a good meal; we had many good cooks in the family and many good talkers. Franklin was both. Now he was married to a woman that runs a restaurant. That is ironic. I did miss the conversations with Franklin, not to mention Maureen's cooking.

I was glad when I got across the Bitterroot Mountains and into the relatively small hills of Idaho. To think, just a few months ago, I had never been on a train, had never seen an Indian, and never had set eyes on a mountain. I feel blessed that I have been able to take in these experiences. I will be glad to share my stories some day with my kinfolk.

I rode through a little village called Mullan and decided to keep going, as there couldn't be more than ten people living there. I keep thinking back to Missoula and the beauty of that area.   Maybe I should have abandoned my search and been satisfied starting a life with my family in Missoula. But I love the area that I am riding through. There are large hills covered with pine trees. The hills are maybe five or six hundred feet high. From a distance the hills are so lush they look like green velvet. I soon entered a small town that I discovered was named Wallace. It was a picturesque little place and I really liked the town. It was in a small valley, surrounded on all sides with hills. It had a river that ran right through town. I decided I would spend some time here in this area.

I checked into a room at the Shoshone Hotel. I found this to be a very nice hotel but a little high priced. They charged me fifteen dollars for a night and then asked me if I wanted a female companion for an extra fifteen. I declined the extra amenities. The room was clean and well furnished but I could not afford to stay here too long at that cost per night. The following day I scouted around the area and found a rooming house that had a room for fifteen dollars for the entire week. I told the owner I would take a room for at least two weeks.

When I brought my things over to the rooming house from the hotel, I met a man named Parnell that was also staying at the rooming house. Parnell was a drifter that had moved here several months ago. He told me about how he planned to homestead a piece of property on the Coeur D'Alene River. All that needed to be done to stake a claim area was to place markers on the borders of the property of interest and have your claim recorded at the local recorder's office for a small fee. Then to get a property deed you needed to build and maintain a permanent dwelling on the property plus cultivate an annual garden on the property. When the land has been lived on and maintained for five consecutive years: you would receive a deed for the property. Isn't America great? Wow, that is such a bargain.

I did not forget the reason I had come almost two thousand miles. The name Bart Decker keeps ringing in my ears. Finding Bart Decker was why I had come this far. I asked Mr. Parnell if he had ever heard the name. He told me he had not. He agreed to ask around and I was going to also ask others if they were familiar with the man I had come so far to find.

In the following two weeks I travelled to many mining towns in the area. I went to Kellogg, Silverton, Osburn, Murray and Prichard, talking to miners all along the way. No one had ever heard of a man named Bart Decker. I was a little disappointed since back in Montana I had found it much easier to find out about Bart and Bull. Maybe Bull was the memorable one of the duo or maybe Bart was dead. Living a life like Bart did could lead to a premature grave.

While I was up in the mining area near a place called Prichard, I really found the area to be of extreme beauty. The hills surrounded me and the North Fork of the Coeur D'Alene River wound its way through the hills like a blue ribbon that had floated down from the sky. I also noticed that the gravel base of the river was a good indicator of a potential mining opportunity. I kept this area in the back of my mind as I remembered what Parnell had told me about homesteading.

I had no luck in further travels around the mining districts. Bart Decker was unknown to anyone. It entered my mind that Bull Lukas may have led me astray concerning Bart's location. I am a pretty good judge of character, and I just didn't believe that Bull was lying to me. That leaves the possibility that I may never locate the man I had travelled the country to find. I would have to readjust my thinking to deal with this possibility. Was I being obsessive about hunting this man down? Some would say "Yes". After all, I had no real connection to my father. Maybe what I was looking for was some kind of connection.

I remember the day well when I went riding up the North Fork of the Coeur D'Alene River. I had ridden about ten miles north of Prichard following this river. I rounded a bend in the river and there on the bank of the river was a great bald eagle feeding on a fish. There was a large flatland area on the north side of the river. Large hills surrounded me on all sides and I got a feeling I had never experienced before. A peaceful feeling flooded my body.

I dismounted my horse and stood watching the eagle devour the fish. I lost track of time but at some point the eagle lifted off of the ground and soared high up onto a dead branch of a lodgepole pine tree. I rode along the river bank to the place where the eagle had been feeding. I looked around the surrounding area. A small creek came from between two of the hills and ran into the river near the flatland area. I got down from my horse and went over to the mouth of the small creek to get a drink. I saw a glittering of yellow color in the gravel. I reached into the gravel and pulled up a handful. I placed my hand in the water and gently swirled the gravel in my hand. As the top layer of lighter sand and gravel washed away, I saw the sparkling rocks at the bottom. I picked one up. It was a nugget about as big as a kernel of corn. It was bright yellow and sparkled in the sunlight. It was a nugget of gold!! Could panning be any easier, I thought? If I could get a gold nugget just by taking a handful of gravel out of this river, how easy would it be to get more if I had the right equipment?

I looked around again. I had passed no cabins, no people, and just a lone eagle in the last five miles. Is this what destiny is; finding something that you were not looking for without ever searching? Had fate brought me here? I sat down on the river bank and took in the beauty of this magnificent vista. The gurgling of the water as the river ran past me, swirling around and over boulders and rocks, was a peaceful relaxing sound. The eagle had left the tree branch and was now soaring high overhead. He screeched as he glided and turned, riding the winds that wafted through the hills. It hit me square in the forehead. This was a place of providence. It is where I am meant to be. I will homestead this land.

Chapter 21   Carl Dunston

Carl Dunston (the old Bart Decker) and Leif Peterson became partners in the purchase of a large two story building in downtown Wallace. The owner had a grocery and general store that he operated out of the building. He and his family lived on the second floor. Leif had persuaded the family that Wallace was not a good place for a family to live. There were big bad miners and lumberjacks and a majority of the female population consisted of ladies of the evening. Carl paid the grocer five hundred dollars for the building and immediately hired carpenters to begin building individual rooms inside. They were able to build seven rooms on the ground floor and eight rooms in the upstairs. Each room had a bed, small dresser and a sink. There were two bathrooms downstairs and two upstairs. Within two months of buying the property, Carl and Leif opened the Shoshone Hotel.

The opening of the Shoshone was a success from the start. Many miners coming to the area had often passed through not wanting to pay twenty-five dollars a night. Now they had a place to stay for ten dollars a night which was still a lot, but many were willing to pay the comparatively smaller amount.

Jack Warden, the owner of the Wallace Hotel and Coeur D'Alene Inn was not happy with the competition. He and several of his employees went over to discuss with Carl and Leif how it would be in their best interest to raise their prices.

Residency in his hotels had dropped fifty percent since the Shoshone Hotel opened.

Carl had been expecting a visit and asked Leif to bring six of his lumberjack friends into the hotel. When Jack Warden and company walked into the Shoshone, the man at the front desk rang a bell that warned Carl trouble was coming. The desk clerk asked Warden and his men.
"Can I help you?"
The reply was.
"Not as much as we're going to help you."
They walked past the desk towards Carl Dunston' office.
"Hey, wait a minute. You can't just walk in there."
The clerk said.
One of the men with Warden gave the clerk a shove in the chest and knocked him to the floor.
"Stay there unless you want more of the same." The man sneered.

When Jack Warden pushed open Carl's office door he was shocked. Carl stood there with a double barrel shotgun pointed directly at the doorway. Leif and three large men were on Carl's left and three other men were on his right. Carl smiled.
"You need to learn some manners, Mister Warden. Try knocking on the door next time."
Warden, although surprised, took another couple steps into the room that allowed the four men with him to enter the door.
"Don't think you can scare me off, Dunston. I've dealt with tougher men than you, and my people are not intimidated by a bunch of riff-raff."
Leif took offense at being called riff-raff and stepped toward Warden. Carl put out his arm in front of Leif.

"Hold on Leif. Let's hear what the whore house owner has to say."

Leif smiled a menacing smile and said.

"You heard the man, Warden. What do you got to say? And by the way, if you ever call me and my men riff-raff again, I'll show you what lumberjacks do. I'll cut you down to size."

Warden, not fazed by the threat, went on.

"Look here, Dunston. If the two of us work together in this business we can make a lot more money together than if we fight each other. How about we combine forces and come up with a daily rate that will satisfy both of our businesses."

Carl looked to Leif.

"What do you think partner? Should we raise our rates so this snake can make more money?"

Leif replied.

"Let me see. Our rooms are full and his rooms are half full. Who will stand to make more money if we raise our rates to match his? Oh,----He will. It's time to finish our little business meeting. Warden, you're done here. Get out."

Leif and his men stepped forward. Warden and his men took a step back while Warden tried to regain his initiative.

"Don't be a fool, Dunston. You won't last in this town."

"We'll see about that." Carl answered.

After Jack Warden left the office, Leif said to Carl.

"We gotta watch them. They're going to try something to put us out of business.

"You can bet on that, Leif." Carl replied. "What do you think we should do?"

"I think we need to put guards around this place. Maybe put someone on the roof and someone in back; especially after it gets dark out. I'll take care of it." Leif stated.

"Good enough. Everyone keep your eyes and ears open. Let me know if something happens."

Around midnight two nights later, Leif was on the roof of the Shoshone Hotel when he saw two men walking down an alleyway behind the hotel. They were keeping to the shadows and obviously trying to stay hidden. They were carrying a bucket. When they got to the back of the hotel, Leif saw instantly what they were going to do. The bucket must have contained kerosene. They started to pour the liquid on the side of the building. That's when Leif raised his rifle. He yelled in a loud voice down to the two men.

"The first one of you to light a match will be dead, and the other will follow him shortly thereafter."

The men were surprised by the voice and dropped the bucket. By that time one of Leif's men came out of the back door with a pistol pointed at the two.

"Hello men. Mr. Warden send you?"

Leif had come down from the roof and met up with his man in the alley. He picked up the bucket.

"I have a message for you to take back to Warden."
He hit the first man square in the face with the bucket. The man went down like a sack of rocks. The second man started to run but Leif's man grabbed him.

"We'll let one of you be able to talk to Warden when you get back."
Leif swung a lumberjack like hammer blow into the man's midsection and doubled him over. Leif snarled.

"If I ever see either of you in this town again, it will be the last time. Do you understand me?"
They both nodded. Leif shoved them both down the alley.

"And tell you boss he will pay for this fiasco."

Jack Warden was not one to give up easily. He hadn't gotten to be rich by being stupid. He hired several more men that had some experience dealing with violence. They were gunslingers. Jack told them to do what they had to do to get Carl Dunston and Leif Peterson to close the Shoshone Hotel.

One of Leif's men was found murdered in his cabin the next week. Leif knew exactly what was happening. They were going to pick off his men one by one until the others became too scared to work for him. Leif now understood why Carl had partnered with him.

Jack Warden was a creature of habit. Every Friday night, he would go up to Murray, Idaho to play cards with a group of his friends. Leif Peterson was also a man of habit. His habit was that he never let anyone get away with harming one of his friends. Leif was also a very creative man. He had done a lot of bear trapping in his life. He built a live trap for bear near the road to Murray. He baited the trap and checked it every day. He caught a small black bear the first night, but that isn't what he was looking for. He rebaited the trap and waited again. The next night trap was empty. The third night he found what he wanted. A grizzly had taken the bait and was in the trap, a very large grizzly. It was Wednesday night.

Friday night, Jack Warden was riding to Murray for his weekly card game. The sun was just above the trees and was shining right in Jack's face. A shot rang out. Warden's horse bolted forward at a full gallop. Warden didn't see the rope strung across the trail. It caught him chest high, flinging him backwards off of his horse. The horse kept going but Warden hit the ground hard. It knocked the breath out of him. He heard a bellow come from the woods to his left and he struggled with a gasp to take one of his last breaths. Out of the woods came a grizzly that hadn't eaten in three days. Right in front of the grizzly was a man writhing on the ground. The giant bear charged at the man and the man screamed.

When Jack Warden didn't show up at his card game but his horse did, his friends knew something was wrong. They got on their horses and backtracked the road. They had gone about two miles when one of them spotted a large piece of a torn jacket in the road. They dismounted and immediately saw red pools of blood by the remnants of the jacket. One of them examined the ground and said.

"There's bear prints over here. Look."
The others gathered around and agreed.
"That ain't no little bear either."
They saw drag marks also. They all got rifles from their saddles and then followed the drag marks.
"Oh crap. One man said."
He stepped over and retched on the ground.
"Holy Moley." Another said.
There, about fifteen feet into the woods, was the remnants of what roughly speaking looked like a man. It was what remained of Jack Warden.
"That had to be a grizzly to do this. Ain't no black bear that would have done this. It must have spooked his horse and he was thrown off. Then the bear must have gone after him. We got a man eater loose in these woods" One of the men declared

The men made a solemn trip into Wallace to inform Nancy Warden that her husband had been killed by a rogue grizzly.

Chapter 22   North Fork

F ranklin and Maureen lived in the house with Patricia McMillan in Missoula. The Hellgate Restaurant was a culinary and financial success. Word of mouth reviews spread throughout the county. Franklin's building business was thriving as well as the restaurant. There was a great demand for homes in Missoula as the trains from the east brought more and more people into the Montana land of abundant resources. There was gold, copper, silver, timber and lots of land. People swarmed the area to strike it rich. When the gold bug waned, they found other industries to support them. There was a monumental smelter being built in a town named Anaconda. The demand for railroad ties, homes and mining timber resulted in many hills being clear-cut for the lumber. Bull Lukas was also a busy and successful man, supplying this huge demand. Schools needed teachers. Towns needed leaders to control the growth and uphold the laws. Everyone needed food, clothing and the basic essentials in order to live.

Missoula was the link to the Pacific Northwest and the place to go for those that had been depleted by the gold rushes in Helena, Virginia City, Butte and beyond. Franklin's business became an industry named Miller Building and Supply. Franklin knew that transporting furniture across the country was an expensive ordeal. So in addition to his building company, he began a shop to build furniture: tables, chairs, sofas, cabinets, desks, and bookcases. Franklin and Maureen were financially at the top of the food chain in Missoula.

Bull Lukas was also comfortable and thriving with his sawmills business. He had twenty employees that helped him operate the company. Bull and Abigail often went to the Hellgate Restaurant and met with Franklin and Maureen for meals. They became friends. Bull was continuously apologizing for his being involved with Bart Decker's misdeeds. Franklin told him that it was forgotten and forgiven.

Franklin was becoming worried that he had not heard anything from Chauncey since he left for Idaho. He did not know exactly where Chauncey had settled or if he had established himself anywhere. Since hearing all of the stories that Bull told him about Bart, he worried that maybe Chauncey had found Bart Decker and did not survive the meeting. Franklin decided that he had to take a train trip to Idaho and see if he could find his brother. He talked it over with Maureen and decided to leave the following week.

The first stop that the train made after Missoula, was in Wallace Idaho. Franklin got off the train and checked into the nearest hotel. The desk clerk at the Shoshone Hotel did not recognize the name Chauncey Miller. Franklin checked in the hotel and went out for a bite to eat. There were few restaurants in the town. It appeared that there were more bars than people. He finally found a café where he got a sandwich and a coffee. There was a table of old men next to Franklin. He heard them talking about mining and problems with mine owners. He asked one of the men if he knew a man named Chauncey Miller. The man told him he did not, but one of the other men replied.

"Yeah, I know Chauncey. He lives in a rooming house over on Cedar Street."

Franklin thanked the man and asked him for directions to Cedar Street. He left the café and followed the man's directions to the rooming house on Cedar Street. Chauncey was not at the house. Franklin talked to a man by the name of Parnell. He told Franklin that Chauncey was up at his property north of Prichard.

"Where is Prichard?" Franklin inquired.

Parnell gave directions to Franklin about how to get to Prichard. From Wallace he was told to follow the North Fork of the Coeur D'Alene up stream about ten miles. His property will be on a flat area on the north bank of the river.

"There you will find Chauncey if he ain't worked himself to death." Parnell laughed.

Since it was getting to be late afternoon, Franklin waited until the following morning to get a horse and head up to Prichard. He obtained a horse from the local livery, packed a lunch and headed north along the river.

Chapter 23   The Visit

My first claim (you had to list three choices) for the property that I wanted up on the North Fork was filed and accepted by the Coeur D'Alene claims office. It was the site where I had seen the eagle feeding. I was working on clearing some trees from the area where I had determined I would build a cabin. It was fifty feet or more from the north bank of the river. The river at this spot flowed directly west to east. My cabin would be sheltered on the north side by a large five to six hundred foot high hill. The land rose about fifteen feet above the river to where the cabin would be placed.

I had already cleared a substantial area where I would be able to plant a garden. A small stream ran from the base of the hill behind the cabin and ran into the river just west of where I planned to have the garden. I had already decided that there would not be enough time to build a cabin this year as the fall was approaching and I did not think I could complete the cabin before the snows came. I did not wish to camp out in the snow while having to work all day. Waiting until spring would give me plenty of time to draw up plans and cut trees that would be the best for building.

I learned that there were two species of trees that would be suitable for the structure. One was the lodgepole pine which was plentiful around the river. The other was the western red cedar which would be my preference because it resisted rotting. I began measuring trees with a template I made. I would find all of the trees of a specific circumference that would be optimum for the cabin. Then I would fell and debark all of them to prepare for next spring.

Mid morning while I was debarking a cedar tree, I heard someone singing. The song was "Oh Susanna". That was a song my brother Franklin always sang, mostly off key. But Franklin was in Missoula and he wouldn't know how to find me. As the singing got louder, I realized that I recognized the off pitch voice---it WAS Franklin.

"Who goes there? " I yelled.

"Your favorite brother." Came the reply.

"I only got two." I answered.

"Well there you go then." He said.

I was excited to see him and we hugged and slapped backs when he got off of his horse.

"How in blazes did you find me out here?"

"I followed the smell." Franklin smiled.

"Are you telling me it's time to take my monthly bath?"

"Did you wonder why the flies and mosquitoes are leaving the area? What do you think?" He said.

"I can take a hint."

I ran down the bank and jumped into the river.

"I'm doing double duty here: washing me and my clothes. Are you happy now?"

We both laughed as I climbed out of the river dripping wet.

"I have a lot to show you, Franklin. Tell me how married life is treating you."

"It's good." Franklin said. "You should try it sometime."

We talked for several hours. I showed Franklin where I planned on building the cabin, and where the garden was going to be. Then I said to Franklin.

"Let me show you something."

I went into my camp tent and brought out a small bag. I reached in the bag and pulled out a handful of gold nuggets.

"Oh my gosh!" Franklin exclaimed. "How much of that do you have?"

I held up the bag for Franklin to hold. "Several of these." I told him.

"Chauncey, this is worth a lot of money."

I told him that I had panned this gold right out of the mouth of the creek that ran nearby. It had only taken me three weeks to get all of this.

"The thing is, I don't want to take this into town and let everyone know that there is this much gold out here. Everyone and their cousins will be out here staking claims all around me. I kind of like the solitude around here. So, will you take this back with you to Missoula and cash it in for me?"

"Not a problem, my brother. You trust me to give you all the money back? There may be a steep handling charge." I chuckled.

"Remember, I know where you live in Missoula."

"Right." He retorted.

We decided to head back into town before it got dark. On the way back, I explained to Franklin how I had travelled to all of the mining areas within a forty mile radius of Wallace and not a single person had ever heard of a man named Bart Decker.

"I think I have hit a dead end." I lamented. "The good thing is, without looking for him, we never would have ended up out here. Look at you Franklin. You have a beautiful wife, a successful business and I have this great place that I am planning on homesteading. All brought to us by Bart Decker. I can say that I am a little disappointed, but if this is how it was supposed to be. So be it."

Franklin stayed with me for two days. I showed him around the area and we had a great time reminiscing about all that had happened to us on our journey out west. He told me that he would come back in the spring to assist me in constructing the cabin. I was happy that he offered. Frankly (no pun on Franklin) I didn't know how I was going to get five or six hundred pound logs stacked on top of each other all by myself (other than with a brilliant mind). I told him to bring the money from the gold when he came back in the spring. At the train station we once again said our goodbyes to each other. I was going to spend my first winter in Wallace, Idaho.

Chapter 24   Seduction of Nancy

The word spread quickly that Jack Warden had been attacked and killed by a rogue grizzly bear. There was a large funeral held in Wallace that was attended by most people in the town. Carl Dunston attended the funeral but Leif Peterson did not. Carl made it a point to mingle and meet people at the funeral. He especially focused on meeting with the widow of Jack Warden. She would now be the sole owner of the Coeur D'Alene Inn and Wallace Hotel. Carl was extremely sympathetic to Mrs. Nancy Warden for the loss of her husband. He told her that if there was anything he could do, she should feel free to ask him and he would be pleased to help her. Indeed he wanted to help her with the difficult business of running two hotels and all of the problems that it entailed. He also did not fail to notice that Nancy was a very attractive woman.

The gunslingers Jack Warden had hired to intimidate Carl Dunston departed Wallace when their paychecks stopped coming. Most of Jack Warden's men also were not interested in working for Nancy Warden. Nancy found out that there was one individual who offered his assistance repeatedly; Carl Dunston. Carl visited Nancy frequently and became a friend and confidante. Nancy was flattered by the attention that she was given and was grateful to have a caring shoulder to cry on.

Leif Peterson maintained a low profile during this time. One of his priorities was to discretely discourage patrons from staying at the two hotels owned by Nancy Warden, and to promote patronage in the Shoshone Hotel. He set up incentives that miners would get women to stay overnight with them free of charge if they stayed for more than four nights. He started rumors that the other hotels had problems with vermin living in the basement and in some of the rooms. He succeeded in reducing the occupancy rate in Warden's hotels to forty percent. The Shoshone by comparison enjoyed a one hundred percent occupancy rate. Nancy Warden sought help from Carl Dunston, as she could not understand why her hotels were not doing well.

Carl Dunston was not an altruistic man. If dealings did not benefit Carl, he was not interested in supporting them. Nancy Warden on the other hand was a very compassionate person. She did not have reservations about relationships. The glass was always half full to Nancy. Carl sensed this in her and was able to worm his way into her personal circle of friends. He began taking Nancy out to dinners occasionally. He eventually went to visit her almost every day. A romantic relationship developed between Nancy and Carl within a month after her husband's death. Friends warned Nancy that "maybe Carl's intentions are not so honorable". Nancy laughed at those assertions.

"He loves me and wants to help me." Was her typical reply.

Nancy was so certain of Carl's allegiance to her; she asked him if he would aid her with the hotels and help her improve their success. Carl at first told her that he did not know what to do to help her hotels, but after a little more motivation by Nancy in ways only Nancy could; Carl offered to invest five thousand dollars in upgrades to the hotels. Nancy was impressed by Carl's offer. Carl spent the money to buy new furniture and install new carpeting in Nancy's two hotels. He also convinced Nancy to reduce the nightly rates to fifteen dollars a night. He also raised the rates at the Shoshone Hotel to fifteen dollars a night.

Carl was not satisfied however; he rarely liked to give away money without getting something in return. Four months after the tragic death of Jack Warden; Carl Dunston proposed marriage to Nancy Warden. Nancy was elated and immediately accepted. Nancy suggested that Carl take a fifty percent ownership of her two hotels once they were married. Carl was reluctant, but then told Nancy that he would agree if it made her happy. Now Carl had his monetary return that he was looking for---and then some. They were married in an elaborate public ceremony that was attended by a large number of Wallacites. The fancy ceremony was the talk of the town for months afterwards. The newlyweds enjoyed a two week honeymoon vacation in San Francisco. While Carl and Nancy were in San Francisco, Leif Peterson was busy seeking out further mergers to bring into the Dunston businesses. The three hotels that Dunston had interest in were now making more money than ever.

The next target that the dynamic duo of Dunston-Peterson desired was the supply stores for miners. Sixty percent of the people now living in Wallace and surrounding areas were involved in mining. Miners required tools and equipment, large supplies of food, lumber to shore up mining construction, clothing, and transportation to haul heavy loads to remote mining sites. The general store was the place miners would go to purchase all of these needs. There were several small general stores in the Wallace area: a large one in Kellogg, one in Osburn and another in Wallace. Leif was assigned the duty of consolidating these three general stores under the ownership of Dunston-Peterson.

Leif was persuasive in getting the proprietors of the stores in Osburn and Wallace to agree to a generous buyout of their business. The Kellogg store owner, however, was not interested in selling his business at any price. He had the largest of the three stores and by far more profitable than the other two stores combined. The obvious way to put the Kellogg store out of business would be to undercut his prices and draw his clientele to Osburn or Wallace. This however would have been a long process and more importantly it would have cost a great decrease in profits or even a loss. That was not acceptable to Carl Dunston.

A fire was out of the question. Too many folks knew about Dunston and Peterson's offer to buy the Kellogg store. The owner, named Mickleberry, made it well known that Carl Dunston had tried to buy him out and he turned him down. People would be very suspect of any foul play that would happen to Mickleberry. Therefore, it would not have been a good idea to make Mickleberry disappear or die. Leif and Carl were at an impasse as to how they could gain control of the store. Leif was actually the one that came up with the best idea.

Chapter 25   Morgan

I spent the remainder of the fall cutting down large cedar trees near my cabin site. I cut them into twenty foot and fourteen foot lengths. I stripped the bark from them with a curved draw knife. I found how out of shape a city slicker is when he starts doing lumberjack work. I had basic knowledge of how to notch and fall trees, however I had no essential muscles to do this for hours on end. I considered myself to be in good physical shape, but I would need many frequent rest breaks in between cutting and stripping trees. I did improve my techniques eventually and could cut and strip a tree in around three hours.

I had discovered an old cast iron stoker rod from an old steam locomotive. It had been used to stoke coal and wood in the locomotive boilers. It was six feet long and of very sturdy. I bought it at the general store thinking I could use it to move logs around. It proved perfect for levering logs into piles. By the time snow began to fly in mid November I had cut and stripped twenty logs of twenty foot lengths and the same number of logs of fourteen foot lengths. These would be the walls of my future cabin.

I reluctantly left my little utopia on the river and would spend the remainder of the fall and winter in the town of Wallace. I procured a job in a local store for a minimal wage.

Chauncey

The money I would make barely covered my lodging and meal costs. I knew that I had some money coming in the spring that would help me in buying the supplies with which I would need to build. I heard that the store in which I worked was owned by the same man that owned all of the general stores in the area and also owned the only hotels in town. I also found out that the local hotels were being utilized by ladies of the evening. Some people said that the owner was the one running the brothels: others said that it was a madam that ran the extracurricular activities at the hotels. The man that owned all of this was named Carl Dunston.

I managed to save a few dollars during the harsh winter in Wallace. I have never seen so much snow in my life. Feet and feet of snow that lasted the entire winter. Back in Indiana we never saw so much snow in five winters. I learned that to get around in Wallace, one needed to have snow shoes. I was chomping at the bit for spring to arrive so I could begin construction of my homestead.

Once spring arrived I found that there was an additional problem. The rivers and creeks were swollen and flooding from all of the melting snow. The Coeur D'Alene River was a raging torrent. In order to get to my property I had to cross the North Fork twice and Prichard Creek once. The river levels made this highly unlikely to get across on horseback. I would have to wait even longer for the river to get down to a crossable stage.

I started out on horseback twice only to have to turn back because of the uncrossable rivers. Finally a month after I had planned on starting, I was able to get to my site. I hired a mule team from the livery to transport all of my equipment, food and goods that I would need without having to tromp back and forth to Wallace for supplies. I found that there was still snow in the woods where sunlight did not penetrate.

When I got to my site, I found the logs that I had cut the previous fall were not covered as they had been left with exposure to sunlight from the south. Truth be told, I did not do this intentionally, it was just luck.

I got a letter from Franklin before I left town. He planned on coming to help me in three weeks. He said he wasn't sure he could remember how to find the site. I wrote back to him and told him I would meet him in Wallace on May 10th. In the meantime I did some additional clearing work and did some gold panning as the creek coming out of the hills had pulled more minerals from the hillsides and washed them down to the river. I did find a few gold nuggets but not as many as last fall.

I found that I needed a pick axe. I had not brought one with me and I needed it to lay a rock foundation under base logs of the cabin to enhance drainage to prevent rotting. I rode down to Prichard the next day to see if I could find the tool there. I rode into town early in the morning. I passed a home where a young lad about ten or eleven years of age was out in his yard playing with a bunch of puppies. He said to me.
        "Hey mister, do you want to buy a dog?"
I looked at the five puppies that were jumping all over the boy. They were fine looking Labrador pups. The mother named Mandy was a good sized dog.
I responded.
        "Are your mom and dad here, or are you allowed to sell the pups on your own?"

A young woman came out of the house and said that the

boy had wanted to raise and sell the puppies on his own to make some money to buy a gun. I asked the boy how much he wanted for a puppy. He looked at his mother then back at me.

"Uh, I think five dollars."
I said.

"How about I give you ten for the best puppy you have."
He smiled widely.

"Sure mister. Which one do you think is the best?"

"I figure you already know which one is the pick of the litter. You can choose that one for me."
He hesitated. I understood that giving up one of his pups would be hard to do. He went over and picked up the biggest pup of the litter. He carried it over to me and a little reluctantly placed him in my hands. The dog immediately began licking me in the face. I could tell we would hit it off well together. I gave the boy ten dollars and said.

"Make sure you treat that gun with as much respect as you treat these dogs."

"I will, mister, and thanks for the ten dollars."

"I live ten miles up the river. If you ever want to come up and see him, you can show up anytime."

"Thanks, mister." Then he ran inside the house.
His mother thanked me and said he probably didn't want me to see him cry.

"He is very attached to those dogs. He stayed up all night helping the mother with their birth. He cleaned them up for her and helped them start nursing. He will really miss that puppy."

I told her my name was Chauncey Miller and that I was building a cabin up by Devil's Elbow on the river. She knew where that was. I told her I was serious that her boy could come up and see the dog anytime he wanted. She thanked me and told me to expect to see the boy in the near future. He will only last about a week without playing with that one. It was his favorite. She told me her name was Gabrielle Nielson and her son was David. I thanked her again and said goodbye.

I came to Prichard to get a pick axe and ended up with a pick axe and a dog. It would be good to have a companion with me during my work. At least I wouldn't be talking to myself any longer. I didn't know what to name the pup but after three days I decided on Morgan. The reason being: The pup was MOR-GONE than not. He found more places to investigate than ants at a picnic.

I got the rock foundation laid down for the base layer of logs. I got the base logs in place and notched them with an axe until all four base logs were level on the rock underlay. That took longer than I had planned. Even though it did not involve lifting; I was able to roll them into their positions.

True to her words, one week after I bought Morgan, Gabrielle and her son David, came up to see him. Morgan heard them before I did and he got extremely excited. I thought a bear or a wolf was coming before they rode around the bend of the river. Morgan was on top of David before he could dismount. It was heartwarming to see the relationship that the two of them still had. I greeted Gabrielle and offered her some coffee I had made earlier. I told her it may be a mite stale by now as it was made at daybreak. She had brought some sandwiches for lunch, so as soon as Morgan and David both calmed down after fifteen minutes or so, we sat together and had a nice lunch.

I asked Gabrielle where her husband was and knew immediately I should not have asked. She blushed.

"My husband left us four years ago. We don't know where he went or even if he is alive. We have never heard from him since he left.

I apologized for asking.

"I am sorry. I didn't mean to pry; I just made a stupid assumption on my part."

David looked down at the ground. Gabrielle said.

"It has been difficult on both of us. It is hard for a woman to make a living in these parts."

"How do you make ends meet?" I said. I stayed in town this past winter and hardly made enough money to get by on what I earned working in the general store.

"I do some trapping and sew skins into coats, clothing and hats to sell wherever I can find a buyer."

I guessed Gabrielle to be in her late twenties. She was tall, and willowy with long dark black hair. She had a tanned and beautiful face. I had already speculated that she spent a great deal of time in the outdoors. After finishing his sandwich, David asked if he could go play with Morgan. I said.

"If you can tire that dog out I have a present for you."

"What is it? He inquired.

"First you wear that dog out and then I'll show you." I laughed.

While David played I told Gabrielle why I had travelled to Idaho. She was curious to know why I had come all this way seeking a man of which I had no real knowledge. I told her that something had obsessed me and my brother to try and find the man we sought. It was not for revenge. It was to deal with the emptiness we both felt in never having a father. It was to see what kind of man took another's life and then seemed to go on with his life as if nothing had ever happened. It was to get away and find that essence of life that would satisfy our yearning for something that we felt was missing. I told her Franklin had found his niche in Missoula. He is married and he and his wife have a very successful business. I realized as I spoke to Gabrielle; the reason I had come out west was not to find Bart Decker, it was to find myself.

Gabrielle told me that she had to get married at age seventeen. David was the light of her life and she would not trade him for all the gold in the mountains. Her husband on the other hand was not happy with married life. He was a nomad. He always wanted to travel the country and see the world: but not with a family. She told me he had left her once before when David was three years old and had returned two years later. They had a rough time adjusting to being together, and he finally took off for good this time telling her he needed his space. She told him.

"Don't ever come back. You've burned me twice and it will not happen a third time. If you show up here again, the only space you will get is between your front teeth."

She was stoic. I saw no weakness in this woman. She was left on her own in a wilderness, without a lot of human contact, and she found a way to make it work. I admired her grit.

I asked her. "Aren't you concerned that David has no contact with kids his own age?"

"Yes. One of the neighbors in Prichard does have a six year old and they play together. But I do realize that I need to be near to a town that would give him more opportunities to mingle with kids his own age. I just don't know how I can work my trap lines and live in a town."

We talked for a long time and she noticed that it was getting to be late afternoon. She called David over and told him they needed to head back home. Morgan came over by my feet and lay down and immediately went to sleep. I said to David.

"It looks to me like you did your job, David. I haven't seen this dog so tuckered out since he came here. Wait here just a minute."

I went into my tent and brought out something I had done while resting between my logging sessions. It was a five inch replica of a grizzly bear that I carved out of cedar."

"Wow." David said. "That is really neat. It looks like a real bear."

I told him thanks, and that I had hoped he would recognize what it was. He laughed.

"I'll keep this forever."

Gabrielle and David got on their horses. As they rode away, Gabrielle turned to me and said.

"Chauncey, why don't you come down to our house on Friday night and I will feed you a real meal?"

"I'd love that." I said.

"We'll see you then." She replied.

She turned and rode off.

Chapter 26   The Card Game

Leif's idea that he had come up with was to engage
Mickleberry, the owner of the Kellogg General Store, in a
weekly card game along with several of his friends. Carl and
Leif knew a man that was a wizard with a deck of cards. He
was quick with a sleight of hand that the eye could not see.
The objective was to get the store owner addicted to a weekly
game, let him win a little, and then make him lose big.

Mickleberry was happy to be included in a card game along
with several of his friends and several people that he did not
know. The first week they played five card draw poker and
Mickleberry broke even. There were drinks and lots of
laughter involved. He had a good time and was anxious to try
his luck the next week. The following several weeks,
Mickleberry won several big pots and came out with a nice,
dandy, little profit. The fifth week they played the pots got
really big; several hundred dollars in each pot. Mickleberry
won big. His total take for the night was over a thousand
dollars. He was ecstatic.

Mickleberry was now ripe for the picking. On week six, the
pots got to be enormous. The luck was not with Mickleberry
on this evening. Each hand that he lost, he kept trying to

recoup the losses by making larger and larger bets. The seventh hand of the evening, Mickleberry had three Kings and two Queens—a full house. A hand such as this was almost a sure bet winner in five card draw. He could barely keep his poker face. He bet two thousand dollars. One of the other men raised him an additional three thousand. Mickleberry didn't have another three thousand. He was certain he would win this hand. He had turned in an Ace and seven and drew the two Kings. He had caught a glimpse of his neighbors hand and thought he saw another Ace in his hand. He was positive the bettor could not have three Aces. Mickleberry offered to sign a note for fifty percent interest in his store in Kellogg for his three thousand dollars call bet. None of the men thought that fifty percent of his store was worth three thousand; so Mickleberry upped the percentage to seventy. They all agreed and the call bet was made. Mickleberry laid down his full house and said.

"Read them and weep."
The others groaned except one man. He laid down three Aces and two Jacks.
Mickleberry was flabbergasted.

"Wait a minute." He pointed at the man beside him. Let me see your hand. The man turned over his hand of two Kings, two tens, and a four. No Ace.

"But didn't you have an Ace?" he asked the man.
"Nope."

Mickleberry had just lost seventy percent interest in his store. He wanted a chance to win it back. Unfortunately the only collateral he had was the remaining thirty percent of his store.

"Tell you what Mickleberry. I'll give you fifteen hundred dollars for the remaining thirty percent of your store." The winner of the bet told him.

Mickleberry was like a fish on a hook. The more he fought, the deeper the hook was embedded. He was sure this bad luck could not last. He signed a note for the remainder of his store for fifteen hundred dollars, with the understanding that he could buy the store back for forty-five hundred dollars, when he won his money back. They played well into the wee hours of the next morning. Each hand Mickleberry would say.
"One more hand."

When they finally called it off at four thirty in the morning, Mickleberry had lost eight hundred dollars of the fifteen hundred. He couldn't even buy back the thirty percent of his store. He lost his store and had seven hundred dollars to show for it.

The report came to Carl and Leif that they now owned the General Store in Kellogg. The man that had won it for them moved to Kellogg and ran the store for exactly one month. After one month he got a generous offer from Carl Dunston and Leif Peterson to purchase his store. Carl and Leif took over the store and consolidated their monopoly of all general stores in a fifty mile radius. Prices of all goods in the three stores went up twenty percent in the wink of an eye.

Mickleberry got wind of the sale of his store to Dunston and Peterson. He had been drinking a lot since the loss. He went into his former store to confront Dunston. He was slobbering drunk.
"Duunnstoon, yoouu stooold my shtoore fuum mee." He slurred.
Carl ignored him.
"Heyy mI'm tawlkingg too you You boooooooooold facest cheeeter."

Carl replied.

"You might want to sober up a little before you start callin me names, Mickleberry."

"I ainn'tt skaared o youuu. Yurr a goolll darrrned lian backkstaaaber."

By this time Leif had come out of the back room and walked over behind Mickleberry. Leif said to Mickleberry.

"Buddy, if you knew what's good for you, you would have left here five minutes ago."

Mickleberry whirled around faster than his legs could accommodate. He fell flat on his face.

The crowd that had now gathered around the three men because of the commotion laughed in unison.

Leif grabbed Mickleberry by the back of his shirt and the seat of his pants. Lifted him off of the floor, carried him to the front door and threw him out on the road.

Mickleberry yelled.

"I'm goona kill yhou thieefs. I'mm goona kill both o ya."

At least fifteen people saw the entire scene and plainly heard the threats.

Carl Dunston had not modified his personality when he changed from Bart Decker to Carl Dunston. He was one hundred percent the Bart Decker of old. He saw an opportunity like a light going on in his head. A bunch of people had heard Mickleberry make a death threat to Leif Peterson. Many watched as Mickleberry stumbled away from the scene yelling, screaming, cussing, and repeating his threats to kill both Peterson and Dunston.

Carl was resourceful. He had connections with other men of elm tree character. Meaning they were very shady. Three days later, Mickleberry was in another drunken stupor. A man watched him in his house until he fell asleep on the floor. He went into Mickleberry's home and found his rifle. He took the rifle and went to Leif Peterson's home. Leif was sitting at a table in his kitchen when the bullet shattered the kitchen window and demolished his life. The man then went back to Mickleberry's home and placed the rifle into the hands of the drunken man on the floor.

Less than an hour later an anonymous report was made to the city constable that there had been rifle fire over at the Leif Peterson's home. The constable and a deputy went over to the Peterson place. They found Leif slumped over his kitchen table, dead as a doornail. It didn't take them ten minutes to go to the Mickleberry home. Rumors had been rampant around town about the threats that Mickleberry had made. They found Mickleberry passed out on the floor still holding a rifle that had been recently fired, and an empty bottle of scotch, both lying beside him. Mickleberry was arrested for the murder of Leif Peterson.

Dunston and Peterson Hotels were now Dunston and Dunston Hotels. Carl Dunston had so much money coming in that he looked for additional places of opportunity to invest it. The trial of Mickleberry was short. Mickleberry's life was shorter. He was hung by the neck the following month for the cold blooded murder of Leif Peterson.

Chapter 27   Gabrielle

I was looking forward to Friday all week long. To build the cabin, Franklin had taught me the rule of 6-8-10 in order to get the corners square. I marked off six feet on one wall, eight feet on the other wall and then I had a straight ten foot long pole that I placed on the marks. If I made the ten foot pole fit exactly between the two marks; the corner would be square. I was able to only get one more set of logs in place for the cabin during the week. The base logs were nice and square, but I was having difficulty getting the second layer set up properly.

I tried flattening the two sides of the logs in order for them to lay smooth on top of one another without gaps in between. This ended up being a more difficult process than anticipated. I would place one log on top of the base log and see large gaps. I would remove the log and scrape the log to eliminate the gaps.   This was more time consuming than cutting the logs in the first place. I was becoming frustrated. By the time I started making progress it was Friday.

The entire day I seemed to be preoccupied. I finally got the second layer in place. The only gaps were very small and manageable in my opinion. Maybe when Franklin got here he would have a helpful solution. But it was getting to be afternoon. What time should I go? Gabrielle never told me a time. I guessed that mid afternoon would be a good time. So I washed up, put on a clean shirt and trousers and headed out to Prichard. Morgan ran alongside my horse as I rode. He seemed to know where we were going. He did not run off smelling every rock, stone, tree or creek that we passed. This was a miracle. Morgan was behaving.

When Morgan saw David at his house he ran to him and the other puppies that were playing in the yard. Morgan ran into the other pups and they all tumbled head over heels, as they all jumped on one another. David was laughing and having a great time. I dismounted and said to David.

"Hi David, you better be careful or those dogs will bowl you over."
About that time three of the dogs rolled right into David and knocked him over. He fell backwards hard hitting his head on a stone. It began bleeding profusely as head wounds usually do. I ran over and picked David up. I had a clean handkerchief in my pocket that I pulled out and placed pressure on the cut. David was slightly stunned. I carried him to the house, opened the door and announced my presence saying.

"Gabrielle; David had a little accident."
Gabrielle came into the room, looked at David and replied.

"Hello, Chauncey. Let's put David over here on the chair and I'll take a look at that cut."
I thought "Wow" Now that is what I call an unruffled response to a crisis. We got some water and she rinsed the wound with soap. She got a clean cloth and tore it into a long strip. She doubled another piece of cloth and tied the long strip around David's head to hold on the doubled piece. The bleeding had slowed down and the cloth kept it in check. David had not even whimpered. He did say "ouch" when

Gabrielle rinsed the wound with soap, but no complaining at all. I told them.

"I think I would have cried bloody murder if I had cut my head like that."
David and Gabrielle both giggled.

"Somehow I don't think you would." She said.
The remainder of the evening went very well compared to the rough start. David was rather quiet and asked after supper if he could go lay down in his room. Gabrielle was a little concerned, because she said that David was really looking forward to having a man in the house for the evening. I told her I would go in and talk to him. As I thought, David was upset that he had ruined the evening and was also upset that he had not sold any more of his puppies.

"I'll never get that gun I wanted." He sighed. "No one in Prichard wants another dog."
I said;

"What if we take the pups down to Wallace tomorrow and see if we can sell them down there?"

"Do you think we could?" He excitedly said.

"We have to check with your Mom first, but if she approves of it, then we sure can."

"That would be great, Chauncey. Thanks. Can I go ask mom?"
Gabrielle thought it was a great idea and I told her that she was not off the hook, she had to go along.

"I wouldn't think about not going." She said happily.
I went home that evening, again looking forward to the next day. It seemed that my life had just gotten a bit more complicated and a lot more pleasurable.

The following morning I got up and made some coffee before heading back down to Prichard. When I got there, Gabrielle had fixed a breakfast of buckwheat pancakes and bacon. I told her that the meal last night was better than I had eaten in a long time.

"And the breakfast tops that."
She laughed.

"You just haven't had any of my chicken soup yet. David tells me it is terrible."

We left for Wallace after washing up the breakfast dishes. It was a short ride down to Wallace and when we got there, I suggested that we stop at the rooming house that I had stayed in during the winter. My friend, Parnell, was there sitting on the porch. I had two of the pups squealing in a pack on my horse, and Gabrielle had two of the others. David carried Morgan along with him on his horse. The pups were not happy to be confined in the packs. They were yelping, whining and trying to get out. When I saw Parnell, I said to him.

"Parnell, you really need a dog around to keep you company since I am not around to entertain you any longer."
Gabrielle looked at me like I had said a terrible thing. Parnell let out a hearty guffaw and said.

"How'd you know I wanted to buy a dog, Chauncey?"
David looked at me like I was Merlin the magician. Parnell asked how much for the runt of the litter.

"I always pull for the little ones." He said.
David replied.

"They are fi---"
I interrupted.

"A special deal for you, Parnell. He'll sell you the runt for ten dollars.

"Whoa. That must be one special pup for ten dollars."

"Only the best for you, Parnell." I said.
Parnell said he knew several other families with children in town that just may be interested in buying a pup. By two in

the afternoon, we had sold all of the puppies. To keep David from going into a major depression about all of the pups being gone, I told him.

"Why don't we go over to the general store and look at rifles?"
        "Really; can we, is that OK mom if we do that?" David asked.
        "Sure honey, you earned your money so let's go look for that rifle."

The three of us went to the general store and browsed in the firearms department. They had several rifles. All but one, were larger caliber rifles. I thought that a 30-30 or 30-06 was a little too much gun for a boy; so we looked at a .22. They had a nice Marlin lever action Model 1891. It was a beauty with a walnut stock. It was just perfect for a first gun. It had a 24 inch barrel and held 19 long rifle cartridges. The only problem was the cost. The store was asking twenty nine dollars. I knew for a fact that it was normally less than twenty. We haggled a little and got the price to a more reasonable twenty five dollars. With several boxes of cartridges, David ended up spending thirty dollars. David was ecstatic. He wanted to go try it out immediately. Gabrielle and I convinced him that we would promise to let him target shoot as soon as we got back to her house.

We headed back to Gabrielle's house and as soon as we got there David was off his horse and running into the house to find some old empty tin cans to shoot at. When he came back out Gabrielle had a little talk with him.

        "David, this is a dangerous weapon. You never point it in anger. When you are walking with it you keep the chamber empty until you are ready to shoot and you always carry it pointed down at the ground. You never ever point it at something you don't intend to shoot or you don't know for sure what it is you are shooting at. If you fail to follow these directions, you will no longer be able to use the gun. Remember that one mistake can make a lifetime of regret."

"I understand, Mom." David told her.

David went out behind the house and set a tin can on an old tree stump and walked back twenty paces. I loaded four cartridges into the rifle and handed it to David. He lowered the lever action and chambered the first bullet. I told him.

"Aim the rifle above the target and lower it slowly until the middle of the can aligns with the bead at the front of the barrel and the notch at the back. Then slowly squeeze the trigger while letting out a breath."

'Crack' the rifle reported. The can jumped off of the stump.

"Great shot." Both Gabrielle and I said together.
I went to look at the can and the hole was at the top left corner of the can. I sat it back down on the stump and had David try another three shots. He hit the can all three times. This was impressive for a young boy to have such good concentration and replication abilities. I told him.

"The next time I go hunting I'm gonna want you to do the shooting for me. With an eye like yours we could have meat on the table all winter long."

We all went inside and Gabrielle fixed us a snack for supper before I headed back to my site. After David went to bed Gabrielle told me.

"Chauncey, you have a way with David that I do not even have. Certainly you relate to him better than his own father did, AND, you have a way with me also."

I replied.

"Aw shucks, ma'am, I'm just a plain old country boy that

is polite and likes to impress the ladies. Especially ladies as purdy as yourself."

She smiled and as I got ready to leave, she came over to me and kissed me gently on the lips.

"Now that is a going away present that I won't soon forget." I said.

I told Gabrielle that brother Franklin was coming into Wallace the following day and I would stop in and introduce him if that was alright with her.

"I'd love to meet your brother. Is he as charming as you?" She asked.

"He got the looks, I got the charm." I told her.

She laughed as I saddled up and headed north.

Chapter 28   The Sierra Mine

Carl Dunston was the richest man in Wallace, Idaho. He was never satisfied with rich; he wanted to be filthy rich. In order to achieve further wealth; he was seeking additional investment opportunities. He no longer had the strong arm of Leif Peterson to assist him with convincing reluctant owners to be bought out by Carl Dunston. Carl had expressed his remorse at the terrible death of Leif at the hands of that killer Mickleberry. Now Carl was on his own and only had his financial prowess to convince others to sell their properties. The Sierra Silver Mine was on Carl's short list of acquisitions he desired. It was a very lucrative silver mine, but the owner had a bad history of hiring miners that took advantage of his stupidity. They pilfered more from the owner than he obtained for himself. As a result, the owner thought his mine was not very productive.

Carl had information from several honest miners that worked at the Sierra mine that it was a very rich lode. Carl went to the owner and asked him how his mine was doing. The owner told Carl that he wished he had never bought this pig of a mine.

"I pay more in wages and equipment in this pit than I dig out of it. It's eating me alive!" The owner whined.

"Maybe I can help you out." Carl consoled the owner, patting him on the back. "How much do you think this mine is worth, if I could take it off your hands." He inquired.

The owner was well aware that Carl was a very well to do man and drove a very hard bargain. Carl had a reputation of being a ruthless negotiator and a coldblooded bargainer. The owner did not want to make a foolish offer to Carl because he really wanted to get rid of this endless drain of his money.

"Carl, how about I let you have this mine for seven thousand dollars."

Carl just about choked and almost said yes immediately. He had expected the man to say somewhere in the range of twenty thousand dollars. Miners were taking two thousand dollars worth of silver out of the mine every week. It had the potential of reaping at least three times that much a week with some decent and honest workers. Carl in his inimitable way said to the man.

"I understand that your overhead costs are pretty high with the miner's salaries and the exorbitant cost of equipment. How about we settle on a price of five thousand dollars?"

The owner thought he had just unloaded a lead weight from his waist while trying to swim across the Atlantic. He eagerly told Carl.

"I think that I would be satisfied with that offer. How soon do you want it?"

"Today!" Carl responded.

The next day after having his lawyer draw up the sale papers and signing on the dotted line: Carl went out to the mine and made an announcement to all the gathered miners.

"My name is Carl Dunston, and I am the new owner of the Sierra Silver Mine. As of right now, you are all fired. Each one of you if you want; can come and talk to me personally about getting your jobs back. I will be in my office until four o'clock."

Each man stopped in Carl's office to plead their case for keeping their job. Many had families with bills to pay and most of them were willing to do whatever it took to keep food on their tables. Several of the men, however, were very angry with how the new owner was treating them. One man in particular by the name of Rollins, had cheated the old owner by coming to the mine with several of his friends at night and moving ore out of the mine without the owner knowing about it. During the days these men would sleep in the back of the mine, while still collecting their daily wage. All the other miners knew what they were doing but no one spoke up. Carl, however, had found out about this scam and confronted the cheater.

"I know what you have been doing, Rollins." Carl said.

"If I find out you are cheating me I will not only fire you, I will make sure that you won't be able to work for a long, long time. Do you understand me?"

"Don't worry, Dunston; I ain't gonna work for you anyway. Screw you I quit. If you mess with any of my friends, you will regret it. Do YOU understand ME?"

Carl was taken off guard by this. He no longer had his enforcer in his employee. He didn't plan on needing to have a tough guy in his employ at this point with all his wealth and reputation; he thought he could handle any situation that came up by throwing money at the problem. But he wasn't used to dealing with men that literally fractured the earth in terrible working conditions in order to eke out a living. The less they had, the less they had to lose. Rollins had nothing to lose; in fact, he loved making others lose.

Carl Dunston was able to hire twelve of the fifteen men that had previously worked in the Sierra Mine. He hired them on different terms however. They were now going to be paid by the tonnage of ore that they extracted rather than a daily or hourly wage. The prior owner had paid them a measly three dollars for a twelve hour day which amounted to twenty-five cents an hour for the sweat, toil, dust, and backbreaking work.

Now the miners could get as much as a dollar per ton of ore that they removed. Twelve miners on a good day could take out fifty to sixty tons of ore. This means that they could make four to five dollars per man if they all worked together and worked hard all day. Previously, on a real good day the fifteen men working in the Sierra mine would put out thirty tons a day. Now they could almost double their salary if they just worked together.

Rollins, after quitting, had a lot of free time on his hands. He began talking to the miners all around the Coeur D'Alene mining area. Hundreds of miners were getting paltry wages and suffered terrible working conditions. Some of them died in mining accidents that could have been easily prevented but the mine owners just didn't care. Rollins knew the miners were upset with all of the mine owners and he began talking to them about forming a miners union.

The miners in the entire Coeur D'Alene mining district were more than a thousand strong. Rollins began trying to convince them that unions were the way to improve their pay and working conditions. A miners union was meant to consolidate the miners into a viable negotiating position to improve wages and mine safety. The problem was the mine owners like Dunston and the bigger mine owners in the Kellogg and Mullan areas had the ear and pocketbook of the political leaders and law enforcers. The owners would fire anyone that was found to belong to the union of miners. The owners hired Pinkerton security services to infiltrate the miners and find the people that were organizing the union. The organizers would then be fired.

Carl Dunston found that his new incentive for his mine workers had been a success. The production from his mine increased three fold from the previous year. But the miners were still working in unsafe conditions and the pay, although better than with the previous owner, still was miserable pay to support a family. Carl was raking in more money than ever and his reputation as a business man was growing by leaps and bounds.

Chapter 29   Carl Uncovered

Franklin arrived in Wallace on May 10th as he had promised. When I met him there I was surprised to find that his wife Maureen along with Abigail Lukas and her daughter Charlene were with him. They greeted me with hugs and kisses as if I were a long lost brother. Oh, I guess I am. Anyway, I told them I had a surprise for them as we rode toward Prichard and Gabrielle's house. They ask what it was.

"You'll see soon enough." I replied.

Outside at Gabrielle's they saw Morgan and the mother dog playing in the yard.

"This is my new addition to the family." I said. "His name is Morgan and that is his mother."

"Oh, there is someone else I would like you to meet." I knocked on the door and Gabrielle came to the door and gave me a big hug and kiss.

"I'd like you to meet Gabrielle Nielsen. She and her son David have helped me to adjust to living in the middle of nowhere. They are very special people to me. Gabrielle, this is my brother Franky, his wife, Maureen, and our friend, Abigail Lukas, and her daughter, Charlene."

Franklin looked at me and Gabrielle.

"Just let me tell you how nice it is to meet you, Gabrielle, and let me say, I know my brother well. I can tell you without a doubt. He is smitten by you."

Gabrielle welcomed everyone and invited us into the house. She had made deep fried doughnuts sprinkled with sugar and had coffee and lemonade for us. David came into the room and was taken aback by more people than he had ever seen in his house. He noticed Charlene immediately. Charlene was twelve years old. She had long black hair and dark penetrating eyes like her mother. David said.

"Hi, I'm David. What is your name?" She told him her name was Charlene.

"Do you want to go outside and play with the dogs?" He asked.

"Sure." Charlene replied.

They were out the door and laughing before the door closed behind them.

"Well I think we'll have a hard time getting them back inside anytime soon." Gabrielle said.

We sat around talking for quite a while. Maureen told Gabrielle about her restaurant business and Abigail told her about her clothing manufacturing business. Franklin talked about his construction company and I told him I could use his advice in laying logs together that wouldn't allow a bear to crawl in between the gaps that I left. Gabrielle had so much to tell them about her trapping and showed Abigail some of the garments that she sewed from the pelts she collected. Abigail was totally impressed.

"I think those would sell like hotcakes in Missoula. You and I should team up and have a special line of clothing 'Designed by Gabrielle'." Abigail told her.

Franklin told me that Bull Lukas was coming also later in the week and bringing some supplies with him to help us with the construction. I would be delighted to have four more strong arms to help me with lifting and setting logs in place. I wouldn't just have to rely on my mental prowess to build. This was going to work out well.

As we all got ready to leave, Gabrielle said to all.
"If any of you decide that you need a place to stay with a solid roof over your head, you are certainly welcome to stay here as long as you like. I would welcome the company." Abigail told her.
"Gabrielle, why don't you, Abigail and I go into Wallace in a couple days and do some shopping."
They arranged to go into Wallace three days hence.

Bull Lukas arrived the following day with a wagon full of building supplies. Franklin, Bull and I worked like busy beavers and were able to get five courses of logs laid in two days. Bull had brought a wood plane tool that was very helpful in flattening the tops of each log layer so there were no gaps in between them. I was extremely pleased with the progress we were making.

The ladies and Charlene had fun playing with Morgan, fixing us meals and exploring the river area. I showed them how to pan for gold and they actually were successful in finding a few nuggets. On Thursday, Abigail and Maureen went down to Prichard. I travelled with them and brought David back with me to the cabin while the women went into Wallace. David was excited to come with me as Charlene was still at the cabin. When David and I got to the cabin, Charlene and Morgan were waiting for us. The three of them went off to the river to play. I told them to stay within our sight as there were bears and wolves in this area. Their eyes got big and they both said.
"Really!"

Abigail, Maureen and Gabrielle rode into Wallace and went to several stores. They ended up in the general store to look at the clothes they offered. Abigail told Gabrielle.

"The clothes that you sewed are far superior to anything they have to offer in this store. We would do well if we started up a store in this town to offer a better line of clothes. Competition would be a good thing for Wallace."

While they were browsing the store a tall thin man walked into the store and went over to the clerk and began talking to her. Abigail had her back to the counter and did not notice him at first. When she turned around she let out a gasp when seeing who it was.

"Oh my Gosh!!!" she exclaimed.

"What is it?" Maureen asked.

"That man." She whispered. "That is Bart Decker."

Bart (Carl) did not recognize Abigail as she was no longer dressed like a "redskin" and no longer had braided pigtails but was a woman that wore makeup and a modern hair style. In fact he paid no attention to the three women at all.

When Bart left the store Abigail walked over to the clerk and inquired.

"That man that you were just talking to; do you know him?"

"Of course honey. He owns this place and also most of the rest of the town."

"What is his name?" Abigail inquired.

"Well honey--- that is Carl Dunston. He is the richest man in Wallace."

Chapter 30   The Union

$\mathbf{R}$ollins had caused havoc among the mining community.
His union organization efforts had been popular with the
miners but disastrous in the consequences. Mine owners were
adamant about not employing any miners that belonged to a
union or even promoted a union among their employees.
They fired any organizers or known union members. The
union was unsuccessful at breaking the backs of the mine
owners; it was the other way around. The miners were
getting their collective backs broken.

   Although Carl Dunston had not fired any of his miners---
yet; he hired a Pinkerton man as one of his miners and had
him infiltrate the Sierra mine workers. His job was to snitch
on any of the miners that were talking about organizing a
union or already belonged to the union. The Sierra mine was
so prosperous that Dunston now had over thirty miners
working the Sierra and he did not want to allow the miners to
ruin his most prodigious money maker.

   The miners were uncertain about how to deal with the
unfair conditions under which they worked. Some miners
wanted to go on a strike and refuse to do any mining until the
mine owners kowtowed to their demands. Other miners

wanted to launch a succession of physical attacks on not only the mine owners, but on their property and families. A few miners wanted to do harm to the mines themselves, the object being, if they didn't get a fair wage, if the mines were destroyed, the mine owners would not get anything out of them either. There were arguments and even physical confrontations among the miners that caused much turmoil. Indecision caused more frustration and anger.

Carl did not give a hoot about his miners. What he cared about was to continue the output of his mine that was creating a seven thousand dollar a month profit for his bank account. Paying the miners a fair wage would take away thousands of dollars a month from his bottom line. He did not want that to happen. He discussed with other mine owners how they needed to keep a consolidated front and not surrender to any of the union efforts or demands. Carl and the other miners also provided large monetary incentives to the local politicians to keep their support. The mine owners definitely held the best hand in this card game.

Rollins stepped up his union recruiting. It was not beyond Rollins to intimidate miners in order to get his way. He travelled to Mullan, Kellogg, Osburn, and Burke Canyon Creek areas. He recruited many men to assist him in unionizing. Pressure was applied to reluctant miners that did not want to join the union. In the end, almost all of the miners signed up. There were over a thousand miners in these areas. The Western Federation of Miners Union was formed to be the miner's voice. The miners were optimistic that now they had the leverage that they needed to weaken the owners and gain some concessions.

The owners on the other side formed their own Mine

Owners Association. They consolidated their positions of not giving ANY concessions to the greedy union. The warfront was established and the stage was set for a confrontation of epic proportions.

Chapter 31   Carl is Bart

Abigail, Gabrielle and Maureen rode all the way to Chauncey's property. Upon getting there, Abigail jumped off the horse and yelled.

"Bull, Chauncey, come here quick!"
I thought something bad had happened so I ran down to the river to meet them.

"What is wrong, what happened?" I asked.

"You'll not believe who I saw in Wallace. She said.

"I'll believe you if you tell me." I said.
Bull also said.

"Just tell us who you saw."

"BART DECKER!!!!" She said.

"What?" I said. "I have looked all over this area for him. How could you find him in four hours?"

"You didn't find him because he isn't going by the name Bart Decker any more. I found out he is calling himself Carl Dunston now."

"CARL DUNSTON. I know who he is. He is THE big shot of Wallace. He owns half the town." I exclaimed.

"Well, you never found him because you never knew what he looked like, you only knew his name. But Carl Dunston IS Bart Decker."

Bull was silent during this conversation. I looked at Bull and saw a glint of anger in his eyes.

"What do you mean — he owns half the town?" Bull asked.

"He owns three hotels, three of the only general stores in a fifty mile radius, and a silver mine. The man is filthy rich from what I hear." Abigail said.

"We looked in the general store in Wallace and everything in there is considerably overpriced compared to what we can buy it for in Missoula. If Gabrielle and I started a store in Wallace with items priced fairly. We would cut the legs out from under that general store."

"Knowing Bart Decker, like I know him: he would cut your legs off before you cut off his income." Bull retorted. "You would be wise to think twice before confronting that snake in the grass."

"What about a restaurant? There doesn't seem to be a real good restaurant in town from what I saw." Maureen declared. "In fact, I really would like running a restaurant here on my own. My mother is completely settled into the business in Missoula and even has a boyfriend there. What do you think, Franklin? We could build a home in the Wallace area and move here. I really like the beauty of the area around here."

Franklin wasn't so quick to abandon his construction business in Montana.

"What about the Miller Construction Company? I'd hate to leave that right now when it is doing so well. We should think a little more on this before we leap into it."
Abigail Lukas, on the other hand was very interested in leaping.

"I would love to start up a store to undercut that slimy Bart Decker or whatever he calls himself now. With Gabrielle's skills and our business experience, we would have a superior line of goods to offer to the people of Wallace.

What do you think, Bull?

"I would be concerned about Bart's response to a new store in town in direct competition with his. That man is capable of having others do his dirty work for him. I would be worried that you could put yourself in harm's way by trying something like that. But, if that is what you want to do, I will support you one hundred percent."

I couldn't keep my two cents out of the pot on this one. I said.

"Gabrielle and Abigail, I think this is a tremendous idea Gabrielle, this would be a good chance for you to have an outlet to show your sewing and trapping skills. A store in town could put your talent on display. And, there is always the effect of damaging the business of a murderer.

They were all quiet for a long while. Franklin was the first one to break the silence.

"What the heck. I can start a business here as easily as I did in Missoula. Let's see what is available in Wallace for starting a restaurant. Maybe we could buy two buildings and put the restaurant in one and a store in the other."

Abigail, Maureen and Gabrielle were all in agreement that their next trip into town would be to search for a place in which they could locate a store and a restaurant. I looked at Franklin and Bull saying.

"Well I guess we have that all decided now. I guess I better get this place finished so you all have a place to stay for your visits here."

The remainder of the week we spent working on the cabin and it went unbelievable fast with all of us working together. By the weekend we were putting on the roof of the cabin. Had I worked alone it would have been fall before I had this much done. We split cedar for shingles and laid row after row of cedar shake shingles.

Gabrielle came up almost every day to help with the building and other chores. I was grateful that she was comfortable with my brother and the others that were visiting. We all go along well together. Franklin had told me how much he liked Gabrielle and David.

"They are perfect for you." He told me.

"Perfect for what? I inquired.

"You know, Chauncey. She and you are a match like bread and butter."

"A food analogy? Really?

"Come on, Chauncey, you are being difficult like a little brother."

"I am your little brother." I replied.

The three women returned to Wallace and were able to find two buildings that would be appropriate for a store and a restaurant. The owner of the property was somewhat interested in selling the buildings but he wanted a premium price. The next day Bull and Franklin went into town with the women and they again talked to the building owner. His price was considerably lower this time than it was the day before. Franklin and Bull told the women that they would supply the funds they needed in order to start the two businesses. They purchased the two buildings and began making plans.

Bull Lukas, Abigail, and daughter Charlene left the following day to head back to Montana. Abigail Lukas said she would work on selecting a woman in her store in Missoula to take over the daily operation there. When the woman was ready, Abigail would return to Wallace and work with

Gabrielle to start up their new business in Wallace.

Franklin and I put the finishing touches on the outside of the cabin, adding windows, a strong door and building a smoke house/meat storage house in back of the cabin. We made it extra strong to discourage animals that decided to acquire a free meal. We also built some furniture for the inside of the cabin; a table, some chairs, two beds and some shelving for storage.

I had ordered a pot bellied stove several weeks before in Wallace and it was delivered before Franklin left. A wagon brought it in. It was so heavy I was glad that Franklin was there to help unload and install it. I now had a fully functional home, and it wasn't even summer yet. By the time Franklin and Maureen had to leave, I was working on putting in a garden which was a little late for planting. The cabin had taken priority over food. Maureen and Franklin left for their home and I was on my own again. Gabrielle had let David come up to the cabin almost every day while they were here. So on most days there were six or seven people and two dogs at my place. Now I was rather lonely and Morgan missed all of his playmates also.

That afternoon Morgan and I went down to Prichard. Gabrielle had left a note on her door saying that she was out checking her trap line and David was with her. I rode back home rather disheartened. During the evening I was weeding in the garden when I got the feeling I was being watched. I rose up and looked around. No one was anywhere in sight. Morgan indicated that something was wrong by lowering his head and growling lowly. I knew that growl, and it meant there was danger nearby. I looked around once more and I saw him. He was across the river maybe a hundred yards away.

He was standing in the shadows among the pine trees. It was a large black wolf that I could barely differentiate from the shadows. He also had his head lowered in a threatening pose. I could see the yellow eyes staring right at me. There were no other wolves that I could see with him, but I said to Morgan.

"Come on boy, let's head to the cabin."

I had no rifle or hand gun with me if the wolf decided I looked like an easy meal. When I looked back up, the wolf had gone. I decided it was best to get going inside anyway even if I couldn't see him. I was sure there had to be more wolves with the black one; I had been hearing a pack howling on several different occasions. There is nothing more chilling or wild sounding than a howling wolf pack, even more so if it is close by. I decided from that point on, I would not go outside without a rifle or gun accompanying me.

Chapter 32   The Grizzly

At some point I knew I would have to stock my smoke house storage building with a supply of meat. I could not ride twenty miles into Wallace every time I needed food. Morgan was maturing into an obedient pup and he needed more food now also. He wasn't so much a puppy anymore; I think he weighed eighty pounds or more. Morgan and I set out one morning around dawn to do some hunting. I had both my rifle and pistol. We headed north up the creek bed that lay between the hills in back of my cabin There were quite a few signs of deer in the area and I thought a big size buck would feed me for most of the summer

We hiked about a mile back into the hills and found thick woods and briars that made it impossible to see more than fifteen feet in any direction. Morgan stayed especially close to me now and did not run off as he would have several months ago. I got to a high point on a hill that had a trodden down animal path leading down to an area of the creek that was about fifty yards below me. I decided to sit on the hillside behind a small bush and wait for deer or other animal to appear.

The wind was blowing toward me so anything below would not pick up my scent. I had been sitting for almost an hour when Morgan stood and perked his ears. I looked down the hill but did not see anything yet. After a minute I heard some twigs snapping and something big walking in the woods. Out of the clearing down below me I saw the largest bear I had seen in my life. Not that I had seen many---but this one was immense. He had a whitish cast to the fur on top of his shoulders; a silver back grizzly. I felt a chill go through me. I put my hand on Morgan's head, hoping that he wouldn't growl. That is all I needed was for him to go charging after that bear as if he could scare him off. Morgan seemed to instinctively know to keep quiet. He stood still as a statue as the grizzly lumbered over to the creek and clawed at an old dead log that lay along the bank.

Suddenly as if he sensed us the bear stood on his hind legs and sniffed at the air swinging his head left and right trying to get a whiff of something. I tightened the grip on my rifle and hoped that he didn't come charging up the hill at us. Fifty yards would give me about four seconds to raise the gun and take a shot. If it missed, I would be in a world of hurt---or worse. Luckily, Mr. Silverback fell back down on all fours and slowly moved off up the creek to the north. I let out a breath. I stayed put for another minute and then left the area as quickly as I could, going the opposite direction of the bear. Hunting would not be successful on this day. Any deer in the area would have skedaddled when that bear was around. We got back to the cabin and I chopped up some wood and stacked it and did some more weeding in the garden.

That night I had been in bed for an hour or two when I thought I heard something outside. Then I heard scratching on my front door. The scratching turned to pounding. I was petrified. The door was actually bending at the top as if something heavy was pushing on it. I was sure it was that silverback. I knew he was trying to get inside. The door began flexing like it was a piece of cardboard. Suddenly it snapped in half and in the doorway stood the immense grizzly bear I had seen earlier that day. He roared standing on his hind legs, he reached eight feet to the ceiling rafters. I could not move. My arms and legs were frozen as if paralyzed when he began coming toward me. I heard Morgan growl and bark. I woke up!! Sweat was on my forehead. Morgan came over and licked my face as if to say.

"It's OK, I got your back."

When I went outside the following morning I wanted to get some salt pork that was in the smoke- house. I looked at the door of the smokehouse and there were deep claw marks on the door. I looked at the sand in front of the door and sure enough there were paw prints in the sand. The prints were as large as my hand with fingers spread wide from thumb to little finger; nine inches across. Was this the silverback I had seen earlier? If it wasn't, then there were two of those grizzlies around that size. This could be a problem, if that bear knew there was meat inside this building, he would return until he figured out how to get it opened. I determined that I would have to learn how to trap bear.

Gabrielle came up to the cabin with David later that week. I told her of the encounter with the silverback and how I found tracks that night by my smokehouse. She told me that her father used to build traps for bear. She remembered the basic plan for how the gate was triggered and how the frame had to be fastened down. She sketched a drawing from her memory of how it was built. I thanked her and said I would have one built by the following week.

I began construction of the trap at a location around a mile from the cabin. I did not wish to lure any more bears near my food supply. I made the outer frame out of logs about the size of my upper arm. I buried the four corner posts a foot and a half into the ground to keep it from being moved. I set the trigger for the door gate and baited the trap with a piece of salt pork. I would see if my trap building was good enough to catch something.

The following two days I went to the trap and found nothing. Maybe I had left too much scent around and spooked the bears away. On the third day I went and found the trap, or what was left of the trap, scattered all over the place. It was literally torn apart. Morgan went up to the trap and the hair on his neck bristled as he growled. Three of the four corner posts were split in half as if they were mere twigs. The trap gate was laying twenty feet away. The sides of the trap were splintered and scattered. I looked for tracks on the ground and found a track, once again as wide as my open hand. This was Mr. Silverback, I was sure. No little bear could possibly have broken the trap to pieces like this. So much for my trap building prowess.

I went down to visit Gabrielle and David. Gabrielle was in a very strange mood. I had not seen her this quiet and serious since we met. I said.

"Is there something wrong?"

"I have some bad news." She replied. "I got a letter from my husband. He is living in Salt Lake City, Utah and he has asked me to come there. Chauncey, I do not want to, and will not go back to that man. He is never going to change. But, I talked to a judge in Wallace about getting a divorce. He told me he wouldn't grant a divorce without my husband's signature on the papers even if he did abandon us. He told me my husband and I would both have to sign the papers in the presence of a notary witness before he would grant the divorce. I will have to travel to Salt Lake City to get him to sign the papers."

"Are you planning on going? I asked.

"As soon as possible, but I need a favor." She requested.

"I do not want David to see him. He has gotten over his father leaving and I don't want to put him through having to see him, and then leave again. Would you keep David here with you until I get back?"

"Will he be OK with that? I inquired.

"I already talked to him about it and he would be excited to stay with you."

"Then it would be fine with me too."

"I will take a train from Wallace to Missoula and from there to Salt Lake City. I think I will be gone for at least four days, if not longer." She said.

I told her to check in with Franklin and Maureen in Missoula when she gets there if she needed to stay overnight. I'm sure they would be excited to see you and put you up if need be.

Two days later, Gabrielle brought David up to the cabin and bid us goodbye. The three of us had a few tears as she left.

"I'll be back in about a week she told us."

Chapter 33   Revenge of the Miners

Carl Dunston was told by his insider Pinkerton agent, that his miners were invited to a union organizational meeting at the local Methodist church. Carl was not happy. He did not want to disrupt his lucrative flow of cash that was steadily coming out of his Sierra Mine. He decided that he needed to take matters into his hands or he was going to lose a lot of money. He hired five more Pinkerton agents to assist him in confronting the men that attended the church where the meeting was taking place.

After the meeting at the church, Dunston was given the names of fifteen men that had attended the union meeting. He called each of them in to his office the following day.   All fifteen of the men were fired. Fifteen replacement miners were hired within three days. The fired miners were irate. All they were doing was trying to get enough wages to support themselves and their families, and assure themselves of safe working conditions. Getting fired for trying to make things better for themselves was not their idea of fair treatment. Rollins met with them and miners from other mines in the area that had been fired for union activity.

Tempers ran hot. Most of the miners were not men with a surplus of moral fiber. Breaking the law was not a concept that was foreign to their way of thinking. During the meeting they put forth an assortment of ideas about how they could get even with the tyrannical owners in general and Carl Dunston in particular. The options ran from: murder, to torture, to dynamiting, or all of the above. The men that had been fired were out for revenge. They wanted blood to be shed.

It was unanimous that the person they needed to make an example of was Carl Dunston: the richest man in Wallace. He would be the best example to use in order to send their message to all of the other mine owners. Dunston had shown them what he thought about Union organizers. Who was better to make an example of than him? Plans were made and miners were told not to discuss the plans outside of this meeting since they knew that Pinkerton men had infiltrated everywhere. The code name for their actions was: "Sierra Day."

There were trains that travelled from mine to mine on routes to transport ore from the mines on the way to the smelter for processing. Miners would load the cars with ore during the day and the train would stop to pick up the full ore cars and transport them to their destination.

On "Sierra Day", as the union men designated it, the miners would get in the empty ore cars and travel to each mine and pick up more miners. When they got to the Sierra mine which was near the last stop before the smelter, they would all disembark and complete their task.

Sierra Day was here and the plan commenced. The train arrived at the first loading site near Mullan. One hundred armed miners walked down the train track directly toward the locomotive as it approached. The engineer of the train had no choice but to stop. He was pulled from the train and the miners took over the operation of the engine and the remainder of them climbed into one of the empty cars. On the next stop, the train picked up an additional two hundred miners. By this time word was getting around to the mines that something was going to happen today. All miners gathered at the mines and as the ore train pulled in with the miners driving, whoops and cheers went up in the crowds. When the train pulled into Wallace there were an additional two hundred miners waiting, and they all got on the train. Along with them they carried several big wooden boxes and lots of guns.

The final stop was the Sierra Mine owned by Carl Dunston. When the train pulled into the Sierra Mine there were nearly a thousand miners gathered. You could have cut the atmosphere with a knife. There were a few mine owners and Pinkerton men around but they were so greatly outnumbered that they knew it would be suicide to try and confront the miners. They were spit at, cursed at and eventually they slowly backed away and fled the area. The miners removed the wooden boxes from the train and told the men to clear the mine. They took the boxes into the mine mouth and five minutes later they came out yelling "FIRE IN THE HOLE".

There was a flash from the mine mouth with a tremendous explosion following. The mine collapsed in a colossal KAWHOOMP! The Sierra mine was no more. There was a chorus of cheers from the throng of miners gathered around. They were all patting each other on the back and shaking hands as if they had just won a war. Little did they know that the real war was about to begin.

Chapter 34   Mr. Silverback

David and I had plans to go into Wallace and buy some supplies while Gabrielle was in Salt Lake City. When we got into town, I stopped to see my old buddy Parnell at the rooming house. His pup, that he called Pepper, had grown quite a bit also. I got to telling Parnell about the grizzly and my attempt to trap him. His reply was:

"Chauncey, you watch out for that bar. There was a man several years ago up near Murray that was killed by a rogue griz. Ya know when one of them bars gets a taste for humans; they will hunt them down like a fox hunting a chicken. In fact several men have disappeared in that area over the years and rumor is that griz may be takin them."

I remembered the silverback standing on his hind legs by the creek and swinging his head as if he smelled something and was trying to locate the source.

"I wonder if that griz followed me back to the cabin and smelled the meat in my smoke house that night. Grizzlies can be totally unpredictable. But one that has tasted human blood will look for more. I guess we must taste good." I said.

"You watch yurself, Chauncey. I ain't hankering to attenda funeral. Besides then I would have to take care of yur dog too." Parnell snickered.

Chauncey

David had been listening and told me that he could take care of the grizzly with his rifle. I told him.

"That .22 of yours would just make that grizzly mad if you shot him. You'd be better off climbing the nearest tree if you ran into him. Grizzlies can't climb."

David laughed, but I could tell that he was bothered by the concept of a rogue bear living up near Prichard.

That night we were back in my cabin and I was cooking up some ham and beans for supper. David asked me.

"Can I see those scratch marks on the smokehouse that you told Mr. Parnell about?"

I took him out to the smokehouse and he saw the claw marks on the side of the building and on the door. The marks reached up as high as the roof of the building. Over seven feet up.

"Is he really that big?" David asked.

"Yeah he is David. But don't you worry, we have a warning system right here in the cabin."

"What is a warning system?" He questioned.

"Him." I said, pointing to Morgan.

"That dog can hear a mosquito flying a quarter mile away." I said.

David laughed, but I wasn't sure I had lessened his apprehension. Heck, I had that nightmare about the monster silverback the night after I saw him. A young lad like David, sleeping in a strange bed with his mom gone, probably was going to have some sleepless nights ahead.

The next morning I took David out and we did a little fishing in the river. We both caught a couple nice trout. I showed David how to fillet them and we had a lunch of fried trout. David was a quick learner. I also showed him how to pan for gold. We dug several shovels full of gravel from the mouth of the creek and we panned it. He was really excited when he found several small nuggets in the first two pans. Morgan patiently watched us as we fished and panned. I was taking his playmate away from him, but he was content to lay in the shade while we were panning. Suddenly Morgan jumped to his feet and barked. I instinctively looked across the river.

Sure enough, there in the shadows was the black wolf I had seen several days before. I said.

"David; look across the river back in the shadows."

"I see him." David said. "What should we do?"

"Let's head back toward the cabin. I've got my pistol with me so we'll be OK, but best we get a little closer to the cabin."

Morgan gave a low growl as we headed toward the cabin. As if to say: Hey I saw him first. You guys don't have to run away, I'll protect you.

That night after David had gotten in bed, David said to me.

"Chauncey, are you and my mom going to get married?"

"Well, I don't know the answer to that David. It depends what your mother finds out in Salt Lake City and what your mom thinks about me."

"Oh, she likes you Chauncey, she told me so."

"She did, huh?"

"Yeah, I asked her if she was going to marry you and she said---'maaybeee. But some things have to happen first'. I said what things? She just said I'll tell you when they happen. What things did she mean Chauncey?"

"I think she has to talk to your dad, and then she and I would have to talk things over."

"What things?" he asked again.

"Things like do we love each other, where we would live, whether it would be the best thing for you. Things like that."

I looked over at David's bed and he had gone to sleep. Thank heavens. That boy asked a lot of questions.

David and I had a ball during the week that Gabrielle was gone. We did some target shooting with his new rifle. One day it rained most of the day so I taught him how to play poker and solitaire. One day I taught him how to navigate with a map and compass. The day Gabrielle got back we were outside working in the garden. Gabrielle rode up and ran to give us both big hugs. I ask her how everything went.

"I'll talk to you later." She responded.

Uh oh, I thought. That is not a good sign. When it was time for them to leave, David said to his mother.

"Can we stay here tonight?

We both laughed and said that wouldn't be a good idea right now.

"Why not?" He asked.

"Because we are not married." Gabrielle finally replied.

Parnell came up to visit me several days later. We got to talking about Mr. Silverback. I told him I had seen more signs that a bear had been around the cabin again. I found bear scat and scratches on nearby trees.

"He may be stalking me." I said.

Well," Parnell said. "We need to get him before he gets you."

We went up to the location where I had built the first trap. We decided that the problem was Mr. Silverback was so big that the gate hit him in the butt and did not close. Once he broke the gate he tore the rest of the trap to pieces.

"He may have been trapped before." Parnell supposed.

We began building a new trap with a longer body but the same width. The bear could not be allowed to turn around in the trap. If it was able to turn around it would get enough leverage to break something. Once it broke one support it was a matter of time before he could dismember the whole thing.

It took us most of the day to build the new trap. We baited it and left for the cabin. We hadn't gone more than a hundred yards from the trap when Morgan and Pepper began barking. I saw the fur on Morgan's neck stand straight up. I started to raise my rifle even though I saw nothing, I knew there was something there.

Out of the woods to our right the silverback came charging at us at lightning speed. Morgan and Pepper both took off straight toward the bear. Pepper went right and Morgan went left. The bear slowed enough to snap at them but he kept coming with the dogs biting at his hind quarters. I was able to get one shot off before he was on top of us. I dove to my left and heard Parnell scream. I landed awkwardly on my left arm and heard a crack. The rifle scooted about ten feet away from my grasp. I rolled over and saw the bear lift Parnell off his feet and shake him like a rag doll. The dogs were going crazy biting at his legs, but the bear completely ignored them. He had Parnell by his shoulder. Parnell was screaming in pain and flailing his arms at the bear. I had no time to retrieve the rifle. Parnell would be dead before I got to it. I drew my .45 revolver. I could not shoot at the bear's head for fear of hitting Parnell. I shot the bear in his right side.

Chauncey

The bear roared and dropped Parnell. This is when things shifted into slow motion. It is amazing how many thoughts can flash through your mind in less than the blink of an eye. I knew that a bear's brain is about the size of a walnut. A bear does not think, it reacts. I, however, was thinking many thoughts all at once. One was: if I die here I will never marry Gabrielle. David will then have the only two men in his life that he cared about leave him.

I knew that I had only one chance to take this behemoth down. The bear still ignored the dogs as if they were gnats. My only chance was to hit the walnut that is this beast's brain with a bullet that was smaller than the diameter of a dime. I pictured Gabrielle in my mind and I wondered why I had been so stupid as to not tell her how I felt about her. When the bear dropped Parnell he whirled toward me as he zeroed in on the target that had just hurt him. He was less than fifteen feet away — two leaps for him. One chance, I thought again. The bear instinctively also had only one thought. Kill him!!

I aimed the revolver right between the bear's eyes as he lunged toward me. I vividly remember seeing Parnell's blood dripping from his wide open jaws. I heard the gun go off and then everything went completely black. I have no idea how long I had been unconscious, but when I gradually awoke I felt warm all over. It was blood; I could feel the sticky wetness and smell the metallic copper aroma. I could hardly breathe as if my chest was being crushed. The bear must have gotten me. How long had I been here? I think I am alive because my left arm is throbbing.

I opened my eyes and saw that the front half of the bear was lying on top of me, his head was on my chest, a snarl still on his face.   Blood was still running from a large hole right between his eyes. I tried to pull myself out from under the monster but I couldn't use my left arm. Slowly I was able to pull my legs up and push my way out from under the dead weight. I heard Parnell moaning.

I went over to Parnell. He was in bad shape. His shoulder was a mess. I saw ligaments and tendons hanging where they shouldn't be. He had puncture wounds bleeding on his side. I tried to talk to him but he was in shock. I ran back to the trap we had built. There were several long poles there we had not used, and I still had extra rope that we had not used to lash the logs together in the trap. I grabbed several more branches and carried them with one arm back to Parnell. I tied branches to the two long poles and made a rough mobile bed. I laid it beside Parnell and rolled him onto it. Parnell yelled out in pain as I could not lift him with only one arm, I had to pull on his good shoulder. I tied a rope to the two poles and around my waist.

I began dragging him back to my cabin. It was slow going. The terrain was rough and I was not feeling so good myself. My arm was in excruciating pain, but I knew that if I didn't get Parnell help, he would never make it.   It was nearly dark when I got to the cabin. I got my horse and tied the bed to the horse and began the trip to Wallace. I got as far as Prichard and knew I had to stop before I passed out. I got off the horse at Gabrielle's home and she had heard us coming. She came out the door and said.

"Oh my God, Chauncey, what happened?"

"The grizzly got us." I said, right before I passed out.

When I woke up, Morgan was licking my face. I won't go into a description of what I dreamed was happening.

Chauncey

Gabrielle was bandaging up Parnell as best she could. She told me.

"We can't take him to town; he will never make it through that rough ride. I am going to ride into town and bring the doctor back out here. You stay here and keep Parnell quiet. If he wakes up, try to get him to drink water. I'll be back in an hour."

I hugged Gabrielle and said;
"I love you Gabrielle. Be careful---please." She rode off at a gallop.

I was having a little trouble breathing; there was a sharp pain in my left side any time I took a deep breath. I supposed that I had some cracked or broken ribs. I gave Parnell some water when he awoke, but he took one swallow and passed out again. The wait for Gabrielle and the doctor seemed like an eternity. David had not awakened the entire time I was there. I hoped that he would not come out now and see Parnell or me in this condition. I tried lying down, but that made it even harder to breath. I began pacing the floor. Parnell was breathing very shallow breaths. I wasn't sure he was going to make it until the doctor got here.

I heard the horses coming up the road. The doctor was the first one in the door and Gabrielle followed. The doc went over to Parnell and examined his wounds.
"Those are some bad wounds. " He said.
He opened his bag and took out some antiseptic and gauze. He asked Gabrielle to boil some water. Luckily it had been a very cool evening and Gabrielle had a small fire in her stove. She put in more wood and set a large pot of water on top. The doctor told Parnell that:
"If you can hear me, this is going to hurt a lot."

Parnell murmured.

"Can't hurt much more."

Parnell still had a sense of humor with all that had happened. The doc told him to take a couple swigs of whiskey to dull the pain. Once more Parnell said softly.

"Now you're talkin, doc."

The doctor worked on cleaning the wound with tincture of iodine and boiled water. He put the shoulder socket back in place as the shoulder had been dislocated and then he sewed up all the things that were loose. It took him almost two and a half hours of work to clean and sew him up. Parnell had gone back to sleep or passed out when his shoulder was put back in place.

The doc then said,

"I need to take a look at you, Chauncey. You're lookin kinda pale yourself."

He looked at the arm and told me it was a clean break, whatever that meant.

"How does that differ from a dirty break?" I asked.

"OH, you'd know the difference, I think." He replied. "I won't have to reset this."

He took two splint sticks out of his bag, placed one under my arm and the other on top, then he wrapped them tightly with a lot of gauze. He then put a sling around my shoulder that held my arm across my midsection. Then he said,

"I need to check those ribs you've complained about, and it will hurt."

He pushed and prodded me in the side until I yelped a few times. He decided that I had cracked ribs and there were none broken that were going to puncture my lung or anything. He told me I wouldn't be doing a lot of physical labor for several weeks.

"No lifting!" He said.

"How about a fork, doc? Can I lift a fork?"

"Nothing heavier, he said; I'm serious, Chauncey. If one of those cracked ribs breaks, you could puncture a lung." Gabrielle spoke up.

"Chauncey is going to be staying here for a couple weeks. At least until he gets that sling off."
I didn't argue. I was pretty worn out from the whole adventure. Doc told us Parnell should be OK. We just would need to keep an eye out for infection. He told us that the bandages should be changed daily and iodine put on the wounds every day. He gave us all of the rest of the gauze that he had in his bag and told us if we saw any unusual redness forming around the wound to come get him immediately.

"The clean bandages are what will keep him from getting an infection." He stated. "I'm going to come back here in two days to take a look at him."

Chapter 35   Dark Days

The Western Federation of Miners Union became known nationally after the bombing of the Sierra Mine. Two men had been killed in the blast. A gun battle was set off between a group of Pinkerton agents and the miners soon after the mine blast when one of them fired a shot. No one knew who had been the first to shoot, but both sides fired a fusillade of shots. With all of the bullets flying through the air it was amazing that there weren't dozens of people killed. Each side claimed it was the other that started it. The result was: two more miners were dead and a Pinkerton man was also mortally wounded. A dozen others had varying degrees of injuries from minor to critical. The county constable called the Idaho Governor who called in the State Militia. Word eventually got to Washington DC about the unrest in Idaho; as a result, the President ordered federal troops into Northern Idaho to quell the escalating violence.

What all of the State and Federal militia did to quell the violence was: all of the miners and sympathizers were rounded up and put in a prison. There wasn't a prison large enough, so the State and Federal troops commandeered a large barn to put them all in. Over a thousand miners, bar owners, and newspaper men were randomly arrested and placed in deplorable conditions. Hundreds of men were confined in deplorable conditions with no sanitation, and very little food and water. Miners fled the area in fear and were tracked down like foxes being hunted by a horde of hounds.

They tracked men as far away as Montana and arrested them; bring them back to Idaho for incarceration. It was a black time indeed for the Coeur D'Alene area, for Idaho, and for the nation.

Without mine workers many of the mines could not operate and had to be shut down. Some owners couldn't survive financially and ended up going broke. Carl Dunston did not go broke but his income was hurt significantly by the destruction of his Sierra Mine. He was told by mine experts that to rebuild the mine would cost more than he would get out of it. The Sierra Mine would not operate again.

Newspapers in the region began to side with the incarcerated miners. Some men that had been arrested had not even been miners, nor had they participated in the mayhem at the Sierra Mine. Days after the incident, masses of people were arrested because they happened to be in a bar or a store with miners that had been at the Sierra. The overzealous militia responded with a shotgun approach of arresting ever one they found and leaving it to the justice system to sort out the innocent and guilty parties. If one happened to be in the wrong place in the Coeur D'Alene mining district they were presumed to be guilty of the mine violence. The newspapers championed the impropriety of what was happening but to no avail. Newsmen defending the miners were also arrested.

Rollins, one of the main organizers of the union, fled to Canada instead of fleeing to nearby Montana. One of his promises as he fled the area was to get revenge on the Mine Owners Association for their persecution of the miners. A few of the imprisoned miners were eventually released; however several hundred were still imprisoned over a year later.

Miners died in less than ideal conditions. The mine owners had won the war and the Western Federation of Miners was broken. Law enforcement and politicians had sided with the mine owners and even passed ordinances to prevent members of a union from working in mines.

Chapter 36   Chauncey and Gabi

I was getting restless having Gabrielle wait on me hand and foot. David helped take care of Parnell and had fun also babysitting Pepper and Morgan. Gabrielle the first morning I awoke after the attack; came to me and said.

"You said something to me before I went in town to fetch the doctor. Were you delirious?"

"I had a vision when that bear attacked me. My life flashed by in a fraction of a second. I realized how I had never told you my feelings for you and if I died, you would never know. I also understood how much I cared for David. If something like that couldn't wake me up; then I might as well be dead. And---maybe I was a mite delirious!"
Gabrielle slapped me on the shoulder.

"Ouch" I said. "Yes, I meant what I said. I do love you Gabbi."

"Gabbi?" She questioned.

"Yeah, that's my new name for my future wife."

"Does that mean---???"

"Yes", I said. "I would like you to be my wife. Oh, by the way, you never told me how things went in Salt Lake City?"

"Wait." She said. "One thing at a time. Yes, I will marry you, and things did not go well in Salt Lake City."

"I'm confused." I answered. "Did your husband, I mean former husband, sign the papers?"

"I discovered that the shmuck has three other wives." Gabbi replied.

"Three!!!" I exclaimed.

"He is now a Mormon that can have as many wives as he wants. He wanted me to stay there and become number four. I told him that a snowball had a better chance of rolling across the Sahara desert."

"So did he sign the papers?"

"He did after I threatened to shoot off his manhood if he didn't sign."

"You threatened him?"

"He was being a complete idiot about signing. He even wanted to trade me a night with him for signing them."

"OK, now I think I will just shoot him." I said. Unfortunately we had forgotten about David and realized he was standing behind us listening.

"Who are you going to shoot, Chauncey? David asked.

"Uh, that was just a figure of speech, David. It just means I was upset with someone."
Before David could ask another embarrassing question; Gabrielle asked him what he wanted for breakfast.

"Eggs and bacon." He answered.
Gabbi told me that she had a message from Franklin and Maureen.

"They came to the train station in Missoula when I was there and told me that their plan was to travel to Wallace in early August to establish groundwork for start up of their restaurant. They also said that Bull Lukas has decided to sell his sawmill and invest the proceeds in a general store in Wallace. He wants to have a store that offers a lot more variety of goods than the current store. He especially thinks that the firearms business would be a big seller if the store had more variety to offer. This means your family and friends are all going to move close by."

"Be glad that ALL my family is not planning on moving here. If they did, the population of Wallace would double." I said.

Chapter 37   Carl Threatens

Franklin and Maureen came as they had promised in early August. They wondered why my arm was in a sling so I told them the whole grizzly story. Pun intended. They were amazed that Parnell and I were still alive to tell the story. I told them I had gone up to the site the day after the attack with a local taxidermist that Gabrielle knew and we found the bear. I paid the man to have the bear hauled out. He would preserve the bear for posterity. I thought that it might be a good mascot to have for Maureen's restaurant or Gabi and Abigail's store.

They told me they had some good news for me. Maureen was going to have a baby and was due in February. I told them that was really great news. I would have a new nephew or niece. I had some good news also, other than surviving a bear attack. I said.

"Gabrielle and I are getting married.

"Congratulations, Chauncey. When is the happy day going to be?" Maureen asked.

"We haven't exactly set a date yet."

They stayed overnight at my cabin and we went in to Gabrielle's the following morning. We all rode into Wallace to work on the new restaurant building. It did not have the view that the Hellgate Steakhouse in Missoula had, but we intended to make the inside of the restaurant similar to the Hellgate.

Franklin and Maureen set up a makeshift bedroom in the back of the restaurant that would eventually become the kitchen. They planned on living there until things were fixed up and/or they found a house, whichever came first. Bull had asked Franklin to work on their store when he finished the restaurant. Bull and Abigail would not be able to come to Wallace until September.

I came down to Wallace several days a week to help Franklin and Maureen. One day I took them to the taxidermist that was stuffing and mounting my bear. When they saw the bear they were astonished.

"Holy Cow, Chauncey! We had no idea that the grizzly was really as big as you said. We thought that you may have exaggerated a bit. This thing is huge."

The taxidermist had done an excellent job of mounting the bear standing on his hind legs with his front paws extended, mouth wide open with his enormous teeth showing in a frightening snarl. He was almost seven feet tall. He could easily reach more than nine feet in the air with his paws extended. When Maureen saw him she became very excited.

"This would be great to have inside the entrance to the restaurant. I think we have just come up with a name for the place. How does the 'Silverback Steakhouse' sound? We could have a motto 'GET A BEAR OF A MEAL'. We were all getting genuinely enthusiastic about the "Grand Opening".

Franklin did his usual remarkable job in remodeling the interior of the building. He built a small platform for our mascot bear Mr. Silverback that made him look even more intimidating, looming over everyone that entered the building. When that was complete, we began working on the General Store for Abigail and Gabrielle. We built display cabinets, counters and display racks. We also remodeled the outside of the building with a brick facade that framed the windows in the front. One day while we were working on building counters inside, I heard someone enter through the front door. I thought maybe Gabrielle had come into town. When I stood and turned around, a chill ran down my spine. Standing ten feet away was Carl Dunston, aka Bart Decker. I debated on saying "Hi Bart" but I decided not to do that. Instead, I said.

"Can I help you?"

"That depends." He answered

I chose to remain silent and let him answer my question.

"The rumor is that you intend on opening a General Store here in Wallace, is this true?."

"My name is Chauncey Miller; you are?"

"You didn't answer my question." Carl sneered.

"Nor did you answer mine." I replied.

Franklin came in and sensed some tension, so he asked.

"Is there a problem here?"

"There may be. Are you opening a General Store here?" He said a little more forcefully this time.

"I fail to see how that is you're concern." Franklin answered.

"Let me tell you two something. I own this town. If you think you can open a business here that is in direct competition with me and my store----it IS my concern; and it will become your concern also." He spit out the last words like he was talking to a child.

"OK" Franklin said. "Now that we have that straight; GET OUT!!"

As he walked toward the door, he said without turning

around.

"You don't know who you are dealing with. But you will."

I couldn't let that one go so I countered.

"Oh I think we do know, and right back at you. YOU don't know YET who you are dealing with."
He smirked and slammed the door behind him.

"Well, that was pleasant." I said. "Bull was correct; we better be aware of what that man is capable of doing."

The following day Bull and Abigail arrived in town. While Gabrielle and Abigail met and planned what they needed to do for the opening of their store, Franklin, Bull and I sat down and talked. We told Bull about the run in we had the previous day with Carl at the store.

"He threatened you?" He inquired.

"I would say it was pretty much a threat, don't you, Frank?"

"He definitely let us know he did not like us starting up a store that competed with his." Franklin said.

"If he steps in that store again and threatens you or the women, I will take care of it." Bull said with a little tremor in his voice. I could see that there was anger welling up in him, and I did not wish to be one to point that out. It was best to let Bull do what Bull was going to do.

Six weeks from the day they got into Wallace. Abigail and Gabrielle opened their store. It was called "Gabbi and Abbi's Place". They had clothing, furniture, canned food items, rugs, footwear, firearms, games, toys, lamps, wall hangings, and about anything else one could imagine. Besides offering all of the clothing that Gabrielle had made, they had a supplier that brought items in from Missoula, and their prices were ten to twenty-five percent below most of the items that were sold in Carl Dunston's Store.

The public inundated the store upon its opening. People came from far and wide to see the new place in town. The sales were phenomenal. Business did not slow down at the new store even after a week. Inventory at the store dropped to a low level because they just couldn't ship goods in quickly enough. People even ordered goods that they had to wait on to get. Carl Dunston was becoming concerned. His stores in Kellogg, Osburn, and Wallace were suffering great losses. Consumers simply did not choose to pay more in Carl's stores for lower quality goods. As quickly as customers heard about the new store in Wallace, they went there to check it out. They were not disappointed.

One week later, the Silverback Steakhouse opened next door to Gabbi & Abbi's Place. Its opening was more successful than they imagined. People had heard the rumors about the grizzly attack on Chauncey and Parnell and that the actual bear that attacked them was going to be on display in the new restaurant. We purposely kept the bear under a tarp to prevent people from getting a preview prior to the opening. Upon the opening, curiosity brought customers in and the food brought them back. People were in awe of the tremendous size of the bear.

Carl was disturbed that his businesses were failing and he intended to do something about it. He acquired two men to accompany him to visit Gabbi & Abbi's. They walked in the store while Gabrielle was working at the counter. The two men went over to a display table where there were three kerosene lanterns on display. One of the men picked up the lamp and said.

"What a nice lantern." He then dropped it on the floor

with a loud crash. "Oh I'm sorry, how clumsy of me." He proceeded to knock one of the other lanterns onto the floor also.

"Darn, I'm just all thumbs today."
The other man walked over to a shelf of canned goods and knocked the entire shelf over causing a loud clatter and scattered canned goods all over the floor.
Gabrielle went over to the first man when he dropped the lantern. When he knocked over the second one she remarked.

"I know what you are trying to do."

"If you knew what I was doing then you would leave town." The man grabbed her roughly by her arm as he snarled in her face.

Gabrielle was not a weak woman. When the man grabbed her by the arm, she cocked her other arm and clobbered the man square in the nose. It not only made him let go of her arm, it knocked him on his butt.

Bull Lukas was in the back room when he heard the ruckus in the store. He went flying out of the room in time to see Gabrielle punch the man in the face. The second man was coming over behind Gabbi when Bull was approaching from behind him. Just as the man was reaching for Gabbi's shoulder, Bull threw a roundhouse punch that caught the man on his right ear. The man crumbled to the floor unconscious. Carl Dunston was standing by the doorway and was watching his men. He only noticed the big man as he approached from the back, after he floored Carl's man. Bull turned toward the door and said.

"Hello, Bart. I've been expecting you."
Bart was flabbergasted. He looked at Bull in disbelief.

"Wha--What are you doing here?" He stuttered.

"This is my store." Bull replied.

"What?" Bart said incredulously.

"My store, my wife's store and my friends store!" Bull barked.

Bart started to say.

"I didn't kno---- " When Bull interrupted him.

"Doesn't matter, Bart. You haven't changed one bit in twenty years. Bullying people and threatening them just to get your way. You threatened my friends the other day. Do you know who they are?

"Uh, the one was Chauncey somebody, the other one didn't say."

"Those two men are the sons of the man you beat to death with a shovel in Indiana."

Bart turned ashen.

"How — where do they---I mean — do they know who I am — I mean do they know I did that? He stammered.

"They not only know. They have followed you for the past five years and finally tracked you to Wallace."

"What are they planning to do?"

"Why don't you ask them?" Bull replied.

Chapter 38   Meltdown

Nancy Warden Dunston was getting concerned about her husband Carl. He had been acting strangely in the last few weeks. She knew that the loss of the Sierra Mine had cost him much financially. But they still had the General Stores and the Hotels. They were still making good money. But she sensed that something else was bothering Carl. He had been drinking more lately and that was not his normal self. She had heard about the new store that was being opened in Wallace but that was only one store. Carl had three stores that were all doing well. How could one store affect all three of his stores?

A week after the new store opened, Carl came home in a highly agitated state. He was pale and shaken when he came in the door.

"What is the matter, Carl? You look pale.

"I uh. Nothing, there is nothing wrong." He deceitfully answered.

But nothing could have been farther from the truth. Carl was shaken by the revelation that two men had tracked him down all the way from Indiana. That had been over twenty-five years ago. Why would they be coming after me now? What were they intending to do? Was his bad fortune recently been the result of these two men's schemes? Carl had never worried about others intimidating him, but he always had an enforcer that worked for him. First there was Bull, then Leif. Now he did not have the security of someone to protect him and his interests. Maybe he should find a new guardian. He poured himself a big glass of whiskey. His three General Stores were not doing well. His customers had dropped by thirty percent since that new darn store opened. Maybe if he dropped his prices by ten percent? He poured himself another whiskey. Bull, that darned Bull. Carl was scared to death of Bull. He knew he could not challenge Bull and come out ahead. He would lose. Bull knew him too well. This Chauncey character and his brother; if they were friends of Bull's, could he still get at them somehow? Why would they be friends of Bull anyhow? Bull had participated in their father's death. Did they know that? Another drink was poured.

Carl was pacing the floor when his wife came into the room.
    "Carl, you are staggering. Are you drunk?"
Carl was now on his fourth glass of whiskey.
    "I ain't drunk. Leave me alone, woman!" He yelled. Carl's mind was not functioning normally now. He downed the glass of whiskey and sat down on the couch. He laid back and went into a half sleep, half hallucination. He imagined himself riding down the road to Murray just like Jack Warden had. (Nancy's husband that was killed by the grizzly). All of the sudden he was no longer riding, he was walking on the trail when the grizzly came out of the woods. It picked him up and threw him to the ground. Carl screamed. Nancy ran into the room and saw Carl was lying on the floor by the sofa. He was even paler now and shaking like a leaf.
    "Carl, what is going on? Why did you scream?"
Carl was confused.
    "The bear attack me." He mumbled.
    "What bear?" She asked, remembering that difficult

day when she learned her husband had been killed by a grizzly.

Carl looked at her as if she were a stranger. His past was haunting him. This had never happened to him before. He never possessed a guilty conscience his whole life. Why did he care now about what he had done to Jack Warden? Or Leif Peterson?. Or Chauncey Miller's father? Or the banker in Kentucky? Or the men in Virginia City? Their faces were all staring at him as he lay on the floor. He remembered that first time he killed the deer when he was just a boy. He did feel remorse for the poor animal. He started to cry when his dad had hit him and said. "Be a man. Men don't cry." That was the last time he had ever cried.

Nancy looked down at Carl.
"I think I should get the doctor and have him check you, Carl."
"I don't need a doctor." He snorted. "I need another drink."
Carl continued to drink; not only that day, but every day thereafter. Those faces kept looking at him when he started to sober up. So he tried to drink them away. They stayed.

While he was drinking himself into a stupor, Carl's businesses were being neglected. Months went by that he never checked on his hotels or his stores. Things began to go downhill on skis. The General Stores were taking in a fraction of what they previously did. Inventories were not replenished in the stores. Conditions in his hotels deteriorated and clientele began seeking other places to stay. Nancy had never been a hands on operator of the hotels. She had left that to her previous husband, Jack, and her current husband, Carl. The hotel personnel began to complain to Nancy that they were not getting paid and that things needed to be fixed up at the hotels. She told Carl, but Carl ignored her. Nancy decided that she needed to take matters into her own hands.

Chapter 39   Chauncey is Gone

I had purchased a home in Wallace to live in during that winter. I had enough money from what Franklin brought back from the gold I had given him. It was over two thousand dollars worth. David and I helped out by working in Gabbi and Abbi's store during the winter. One of the biggest sellers was snow shoes. Franklin custom made them and was able to make three pairs of them a day. They sold as fast as he could make them. Everything in the store seemed to sell quickly. Gabrielle was very happy with the success of their store. Abigail and Gabbi purchased several sewing machines and would work in the back room of the store making custom clothing from material that they purchased and with the hides that Gabbi had trapped. Gabrielle however, did not have time to do trapping any longer. She knew several trappers that supplied her with the hides that she needed to sew jackets, vests, hats and pants.

Business had become so good that the two women decided to hire some more help to keep up with the demand for custom made clothes. The women that they hired had worked for Carl Dunston. They were looking for a job that they could depend on getting a pay check. They told their new employers that Carl would not pay them for weeks on end. When he did pay them he shorted them and failed to correct the mistakes.

We had received bad news from back home concerning our sister, Annette. Nettie, as we called her, was married to Franklin Logan. They had three children in their seven years of marriage. We were notified that last December Franklin Logan had died of a blood infection. Nettie had a one year old named Carter, a four year old named Donald and a six year old named Wilma. Nettie was the nearest sister to Franklin and I in age; we had always been very close to her. It was a shame that she had been left all alone; much as our mother had been when our father, Jacob, had been killed. Franklin and I both sent Nettie our condolences and some money to help her out.

The winter was a fairly mild one compared to the normal. We did not get the large amount of snow that usually occurred. Franklin and Maureen's baby was born in February. They named him Jacob in honor of the father we had never known.

David and I planned a weekend trip to go up and check on the cabin to make sure all was well. We took our horses and made it all the way to the cabin without incident. Gabrielle had stayed home to work in the store. When we got to the cabin Morgan and his mother, Mandy, were excited to have all of the smells and animal tracks to sniff around. They were running all over the area. David and I went inside and started a fire in the stove. We planned on staying at the cabin for two nights. We got our supplies from the horses and went inside. It warmed up in the cabin within an hour. We set up a chess board and played several games of chess. David was getting better and almost beat me. We had an uneventful night. The following morning, at the crack of dawn, I went out to use the outhouse.

Chauncey

David slept in late and awoke to find it was getting cold inside the cabin. Chauncey must have gone outside. David got up and put a couple logs in the stove and stirred up the embers. He went over to the window and looked outside. He did not see Chauncey. He put on his coat and went out the door.

There had been a fresh dusting of snow over night and David saw Chauncey's footprints going back toward the outhouse. Morgan and Mandy were acting strangely. David walked back to the outhouse and saw Chauncey's footprints leading to the door. But, there was another set of prints leading to the outhouse also. David looked closely at the prints. The extra prints went up to the hinge side of the door. He also saw that there was a piece of paper stuck to the door with a nail. He saw a mark on the ground that looked like someone had fallen in the snow.

When he looked down he saw a splotch of blood in the snow. Leading away from the outhouse was one set of prints with the two parallel lines of something being dragged. David ran over to the rail where the horses had been tied. Chauncey's horse was gone. There were two sets of hoof prints leading toward the river. He didn't know what to do. Chauncey was gone, possibly hurt, and he was here by himself.

David ran back into the cabin, closed the damper on the stove, grabbed his hat and gloves and ran back out to his horse that was still tied to the rail. He called for Morgan and Mandy to follow, and rode toward Wallace. He was crying now as he got close to the store where his mom was working. He knew she would be upset.

"Mom" He cried as he ran into the store. "Mom,

Chauncey is gone."

"What do you mean 'gone'?" Gabrielle asked.

"Someone took him at the cabin." David was sobbing uncontrollably.

Gabrielle held him and tried to calm him down.

"It's OK, David. Just calm down and explain to me what happened."

David explained how he had awoken and gone out to look for Chauncey and found the two sets of prints, the blood and the two sets of hoof prints leaving the area. Then he remembered.

"There was a paper nailed on the outhouse door."

"Where is it?"

"I put it in my coat pocket. I didn't look at it."

"Oh my gosh." Gabrielle said when she realized the implications of the situation. "Let me see it."

Gabrielle read the note and put her hand over her mouth.

"Oh no. Oh no." She repeated.

"What is it?" David asked.

Gabrielle ran to the back of the store where Abigail was working.

"Abby. We have to get Bull."

Chapter 40　Captive

I remembered walking outside my cabin and going into the outhouse. I opened the door to leave and---everything went black. I awoke and found myself draped across the back of a horse with my hands and feet bound and a hood over my head. I had no idea how long I had been on the horse, but from the discomfort of my midsection from bouncing on the horse, it must have been quite a while. I tried to recall anything that would give me a clue where I was or what had happened, but there was nothing.

After about ten minutes, my horse stopped. Someone pulled me from the horse and stood me up. My legs were wobbly from the ride and being tied together. I began to fall but I was grabbed from behind. My legs were untied and I was pushed forward. I entered a doorway into a room that was cold. The hood was removed from my head and my eyes slowly began to focus. A man stood in front of me that I did not know.

"What am I doing here?" I asked.

"Shut up." Was his answer.

"Who are you?

"I said shut up. Go set on that chair over there." He said pointing to the nearest chair.

I sat down and he tied my legs to the chair legs.

"Why are you doing this?

No answer. I guessed I wasn't going to learn anything from this guy. He went over to the stove and started a fire. I looked around. The cabin didn't look like anyone had lived in it for a long time. There were several big bearskin rugs on the floor. The kitchen window had a piece of cardboard over one of the panes. I thought I would try a new approach.

"Carl Dunston is not who you think he is. He is really named Bart Decker and is wanted in at least three states. He killed my father in Indiana, a banker in Kentucky, and several men in Montana. I would not be surprised if he has killed men in Idaho. If you have nothing more to offer him than what you are doing for him now---you are expendable and will die as soon as I am out of the way."

"Who said you were going to die?" He queried.

"Dunston, or should I say Decker, wants me out of the way because I am competition. If you are not part of the answer, you are part of the problem and will be eliminated."

"How do you know this?"

"I know his partner that he has known since he was fourteen years old in Kentucky. Bull is his name."

"You know Bull. Carl talks about him all the time."
That answered one of my questions. This guy was working for Carl Dunston.
 I answered.

"Yeah, Bull got fed up with Bart, uh-Carl, and told him he was on his own, he wouldn't do his fighting for him any longer."

"That ain't how Carl tells it. He said he and Bull got into a fight over some woman and he told Bull they were done."

"I take it you have never met Bull. If they had gotten into a fight, Carl wouldn't be around to be talking to you. Whatever Carl has told you; is probably a lie! He only does what is best for Carl. He will get rid of you when you are done with this job. You are just another one of his loose ends to be cleaned up."

The man didn't say anything. I could tell he was thinking about what I was saying. I asked him.

"Whose place is this? I know it is not yours. No one has lived here for a long time."

"He was a friend of mine. Leif Peterson. He lived here."

I was getting somewhere now. He was talking to me and getting scared.

"What happened to him? I ask him.

"He was killed."

"By who?"

"A man named Mickleberry."

"You sure about that?" I asked. "What did Leif do?"

"Leif worked for Carl." He said quietly.

"Let me guess. Leif was no longer of use to Carl."

The man did not answer, but I could tell I had struck a chord.

"Did this have anything to do with his stores?" I pried.

"Uh, Leif and Carl were joint owners of the Shoshone Hotel in Wallace. Mickleberry owned the General Store in Kellogg. He lost it in a poker game."

"I never heard of Mickleberry. What happened to him?"

"He got hanged, for killing my friend, Leif. He thought Carl and Leif cheated him out of his store and he went after Leif. He claimed he never did it, but they found him drunk with a rifle that had just been fired."

Wow, I had really opened a can of worms.

"Drunk huh. Let me guess again. Carl took over the store."

"Yeah" He said pensively.

"What about the other two hotels in town that Carl owns?"

"Oh man." He said. "A guy named JackWarden owned them. He was killed by a grizzly up near Murray. Carl married his wife, Nancy. Oh man."

"Now you understand what I am saying about Carl?" He pondered this for quite a while. I did not say anything for a while either. After what seemed like five minutes, he spoke.

"You really think Carl will kill me?"

"What do you think? Your friend Leif was in business with him. He's dead. Jack Warden owned his only competition in hotels---He's dead. Mickleberry was his competition in the general stores. He's dead. You said Warden was killed by a griz. How'd that happen?"
Now he began talking to himself rather than to me.

"Leif, he knew how to build bear traps. He built them a lot. Got a lot of bear hides here in the cabin. That bear that got Warden didn't hurt his horse. The horse ran off. Leif musta trapped that bear, got Warden off his horse and unleashed the griz on him."

Whoa, I thought. A grizzly that got trapped and released sure wouldn't let himself get trapped again. Old Silverback may have been the same bear that killed Jack Warden. Parnell and I happened to build a trap in his vicinity and he didn't like it. He stalked us after we built the trap.

"Did anyone ever see that bear?" I asked him.

"Jack Warden wouldn't ever sell his hotels. Everyone knew that. Jack Warden was the richest man in Wallace--- until---Carl took them over."
He didn't answer my question. He was still thinking.

"Hell, Carl did not just get the hotels, he got Jack's wife. Oh man. What have I got myself into?"

"You can still get out of this." I told him. If you let me

go and take off somewhere Carl won't be able to find you. Just make yourself scarce for a while and Carl will move on to other schemes."

"Mister, you don't know Carl like I do. If you double cross him he never forgets. I am a dead man no matter what I do."

"Who killed Leif?" I asked him.

"I don't know."

"I think you do know. It had to be someone that was close to Carl and you probably know them. Maybe even a friend of yours. Think about someone that disappeared right after Leif was killed."

He thought for quite a while without speaking.

"TOMPKINS!!" He blurted out. "Mike Tompkins left town the day after Leif was killed."

"If you find this Tompkins guy, you won't have to worry about Carl anymore."

"How's that?" He asked. If Tompkins killed Leif, he ain't exactly going to turn himself in."

I said.

"Think about this. You were friends with Leif. If Tompkins killed him, why would you want to protect him? Tompkins could save his own skin, IF he turned on Carl and told the law what he knows about what Carl has done. Carl is a free man if nobody can prove what he has done. Tompkins could prove that Carl hired him to kill Leif and frame Mickleberry. He may know about Jack Warden being killed also. You need this Tompkins to keep the same thing from happening to you."

Another long silence. Then he quietly said.

"Tompkins has a son that lives over near the city of Coeur D'Alene. He might be staying there. What should I do? "

"Go see if he is there. If he is, then contact a local lawman and tell him what you have told me."

The man opened the door and started out. I yelled.

"HEY. You can't leave me tied up like this."

"Yes I can." Then he closed the door behind him and left.

Chapter 41   Carl Unhinged

Carl was becoming increasingly paranoid. He would walk down the streets of Wallace talking to himself. The most prominent figment of his imagination that he talked to was Bull. Bull would tell him that he was in danger and they needed to leave. Carl would argue with him out loud.

"I can't leave this town, Bull. They need me here. I am an important man here."
Leif Peterson would talk to Carl, accusing him of having him killed.

"I know you had me killed." Leif would say.
"No, No, No Leif. Mickleberry killed you; remember, he threatened both of us. He could have killed me first."

Then Carl would see Chauncey's father, who would tell him that he took him away from his wife and ten children. Carl was being haunted by all of his past misdeeds. Miners, bankers, friends and enemies were all swirling in his head, pointing their fingers at him and calling him---"KILLER, LIAR, CHEAT, THIEF". They chimed in his ears, day and night. He could no longer sleep because of the voices.

Nancy Warden knew that something was terribly wrong with her husband. She consulted their family physician and told him all of the things that her Carl was experiencing.

"You need to bring him in to see me." The doctor told

her. "He may have some physical illness that is causing all of this, but without seeing him, I cannot help him."

That evening, Nancy was serving Carl dinner and mentioned to him that she thought that it may be good for him to have a check up with the doctor.

"What do you mean? You think that I am sick? Or maybe you think I am nuts? I don't need a doctor. Leif can tell you that I don't need a doctor."

"Honey, Leif is dead."

Carl looked puzzled for a few seconds, and then replied.

"I know that, I meant Bull."

"Honey, Bull isn't with you anymore."

"You need to leave me alone, woman. I have a lot of things on my mind and I have the hotels, the stores and the mine to take care of. They want me to run for Governor of Idaho you know."

"Who wants you to run for governor?" Nancy asked.

"The muckety mucks want me to be governor. You know; the politicians. They keep asking me to run. I think I may take them up on that. How would you like living in Boise?"

Nancy was even more worried after this conversation than she had been. She realized that Carl was even more delusional than she had imagined. In fact, Carl began telling everyone he was running for governor. He stopped people on the street and asked them for their vote for governor.

"I'll do well for you in Boise. I'll bring more prosperity to this state. All of you will have more money to spend, and more businesses that hire you. You need me in the State House."

Chauncey

As people walked away from Carl they could be heard saying. "Yeah, I know what State House he should be in--- the nut house in Blackfoot."

Chapter 42   The Escape

I was in one big pickle. I was tied to a chair in a cabin in the middle of nowhere. I had no idea where I had been taken or how long we had traveled to get here. The first thing I had to do was get myself untied. I tried working my hands loose, but the scoundrel had tied them together behind the back of the chair. They were too tight. I noticed that the back of the chair was a little rickety. I began rocking my upper body forward and backward. After several minutes of this I could feel the back of the chair loosen with each rocking motion. It began creaking. At last I heard a "crack", and the back of the chair broke off. I was able to stand up and the back fell away.

The stove was eight feet away. I hopped about two inches at a time and at last got within inches of the stove. There was still a good fire going in the stove and it was hot. The stove had a top that was for cooking. It stuck out several inches to accommodate pots and pans. I turned my back to the stove and inched my way back. I wanted to put the rope around my wrists up to the rim and see if it would char the rope and weaken it. I reached my hands up and immediately burned my arm since I couldn't see what I was doing. I winced and moved my hand until I felt them push against the rim. It wasn't burning my hands so it must be on the rope. The stove was very hot and I couldn't keep my hands that close without a lot of pain. I decided there must be a better way.

There was a box on a corner table by the back wall of the cabin. It took me a while to hop over there. I looked in the box and there was a knife along with other utensils. I backed up to the box and tried to reach in with my hands to get the knife, but it was too high. I couldn't get my hands up high enough to reach into the box. I didn't want to push it further back on the table, so I turned around, bent over and with my chin and gradually pulled the box to the edge of the table. Then it crashed to the floor. Utensils went everywhere.

When I bent down to pick up the knife I fell over backwards with my feet up in the air on the chair base. The knife was close. I began scooting and feeling around with my fingers. I eventually found the knife. I picked it up by the blade and slowly worked it around until I held the hilt with the blade facing toward me. I could only hold the hilt between my thumb and forefinger. Not the best for applying any pressure and I could only move the blade an inch up and down. I tried to keep it in the same position but being unable to see, I just had to go by sense of feel.

For over an hour or more I sawed up and down with the knife. My fingers were aching from the repetitive motion. I finally felt the rope give a little. I pulled apart on my wrists and felt one strands of the rope break, but he had wrapped the rope and double tied it. I still had another strand to cut. This went faster though because it was a little looser now. It only took about ten more minutes and I cut through the last layer. My hands came free. I shook my hands as they were numb and sore. I took the knife and cut through the rope on my feet, and was free at last.

When I went to the front door and opened it, it was pitch black outside. I had no idea what time it was. It was cold out and I had to find something to keep me warm. There were no jackets or coats that I saw in the cabin. I picked up one of the bear skin rugs and wrapped myself in it. I also picked up the knife and went outside. Looking up I saw the most beautiful aurora borealis that I had ever seen. Maybe this was a good omen? There were curtains of undulating green and pink and purple swirling as if they were in a giant mixing bowl being stirred. They were so brilliant that at times I could see my shadow. I spotted the big dipper that pointed to the North Star. At least I knew which way was North, but where was I?

If I could find the river, I could at least follow that, but I had no clue as to which way to the river. Chances were we had not gone across the river after he took me from my cabin. So if I went west, I had to run into the river eventually.

I was fairly hungry since I had not eaten since the previous day. I also needed water. I began walking west, glancing up at the North Star occasionally to keep my bearings. I tried to follow valleys rather than climbing over hills, but the twisting and turning valleys weren't conducive to a straight westerly course. As I walked, I took the knife and slashed a limb off of the nearest tree every two minutes or so.

After an hour I came to a small stream where I bent down and scooped up handfuls of water to drink. It was refreshing, but I could tell I was weak from lack of food. After another hour I looked behind me and saw a slight hint of light in the east. The northern lights had been turned off and the sun was about to rise. I was never so glad to see that daylight glow in the sky.

Chapter 43   The Search

Franklin, Bull, Parnell, Gabrielle along with the Sheriff and four deputies had organized a search party after David had given them the note that had been nailed on the outhouse door. The note said:

"Close down your store, or Chauncey dies."
Gabrielle was terrified and fighting angry all at once. She couldn't believe that anyone could be this stupid to threaten them like this. When she told Bull and showed him the note, he wanted to go directly to Bart and confront him. Franklin and Gabrielle talked him out of it.

"If they have Chauncey holed up somewhere, likely Bart won't know where he is. That will just delay us finding him." Gabrielle reasoned.

David reluctantly stayed in Wallace with Abigail and Maureen. The search party of nine headed to Chauncey's cabin. It was getting dark when they got there. The Sheriff wanted to wait until morning to resume the search. Bull told him otherwise and the Sheriff decided to continue. The overnight dusting of snow had melted as had any foot prints of hoof prints that would give them a clue where Chauncey had been taken.

Parnell was an excellent tracker and was able to pick up some hoof prints down close to the river.

"They headed down river." Parnell announced.

"The problem is our tracks are all over theirs. I'll have a hard time telling which is which."

They rode about a mile south along the river when Parnell held up his hand. He got off his horse and looked closely at the tracks along the river.

"I think they headed east from here, away from the river. It looks like they may be headed toward Little Guard Lookout road."

One of the men said.

"Didn't Leif Peterson live up there between Little Guard Road and Prichard Creek?"

"Yer right. That would be a place no one would look for him."

Bull said.

"Ok. It is too dark to follow tracks now. Let's split up. Sheriff, you and two of your men head up to Little Guard Lookout; he may have gone up there. You three deputies head to Leif's cabin and check that out. Gabrielle, Franklin and I will head over to Prichard Creek and see if we find any signs of them over there. We'll all meet back at Gabrielle's old cabin in Prichard at noon tomorrow if we don't find anything. If anyone locates him, fire three rapid shots every ten minutes."

They split up and rode off into the night. The going was slow in the dark as the trails were winding and steep. By dawn, the Sheriff and his men had arrived at the Little Guard Lookout. There were no signs of any recent activity or prints at the Lookout. Parnell and two others got to Leif's old cabin right before dawn. Parnell was first into the cabin and came running out.

"He was here." He yelled. "The stove is warm and there is a broken chair with cut rope lying on the floor."

Parnell walked while he looked down at the ground. He soon found a fresh cut tree branch lying on the ground.

"He's leaving us a trail. Fire three shots."

They fired three rapid shots into the air and began following the trail on foot with the horses following in tow. Gabrielle, Franklin and Bull heard the three shots in the distance. Gabrielle said.

"That has to be at Leif's place. The Lookout is too far away, we wouldn't hear the shots from that distance."
The three of them rode toward Leif's cabin at a fast pace. After about ten minutes, Bull held up his hand.

"Hold it here." They waited until they heard three more shots; much closer this time.

"Let's go."

They rode hard for ten minutes and paused again. Three more shots came less than a half mile away. They rode toward the shots. Bull yelled. An answering yell came back. The six men met and Parnell told them he found the trail that Chauncey was leaving them.

"He's by himself." Parnell said. "He broke free from being tied to a chair. There was no one else in the cabin. They may be looking for him too. We have to locate him first."

Chapter 44   I am over here

I was getting very tired. I have had no sleep and no food for more than twenty four hours. I need to sit down and rest. I sat by a large cedar tree and leaned back. I must have fallen asleep, because I awoke with a start. I had just heard three gun shots. Someone hunting? No the shots were too rapid. A hunter wouldn't fire that impatiently. Someone is either trying to catch me or trying to rescue me.

The best thing I could do was stay put if someone had picked up the trail I left. I just hoped it was a friend that was looking for me and not an enemy. I stood and yelled.
        "I'm over here. I'm over here."
A few minutes later I heard three more shots. Closer this time. I repeated my yells again.

Ten minutes passed and I heard movement in the woods. Should I trust that it is help or harm? In my condition I knew running would be useless. I couldn't outrun a turtle right now. I stood in front of the cedar and yelled again.

Parnell walked into the clearing in front of me.
        "You look like crap, Chauncey. You look like you were expecting a big silverback to come out of the woods again?"

Parnell said.

"I was, except this one came out of the woods carrying a rifle." I chortled.

Parnell came up and gave me a big hug. He introduced the other two men to me and then said he needed to shoot again. He fired three quick shots into the air. In five minutes Gabrielle, Franklin and Bull rode up. Gabrielle jumped from her horse and ran over to me.

"Oh Chauncey, I thought they were going to kill you. David is worried sick."

The Sheriff and his men never showed up. The others gathered around me and patted me on the back. They gave me some beef jerky to eat and water to drink. I asked them where we were. They told me we were halfway between Prichard Creek and the Little Guard Lookout tower.

"I knew that." I said. "Just checking on you guys."

Gabrielle and I mounted up and rode back toward Wallace. When we got back to the store in Wallace, David, Maureen, Abigail and Morgan ran out to greet us. David was exuberant that I was safe. He was blaming himself that he had not awakened when I was knocked out. He said he should have heard me and come out to help. I told him it was better he didn't. The man might have shot you.

Our next order of business was to file a report at the Sheriff's office about what had happened. The Sheriff was a friend of Carl Dunston and had doubts that Carl was involved in my kidnapping. While I was at the Sheriff's office the telegraph operator came into the office and said he had a telegram from the Sheriff over in Coeur D'Alene. The telegram said that a person by the name of Mike Tompkins had come into his office and confessed to the murder of Leif Peterson. He claims that he was given orders by a man named Carl Dunston to frame another man named Mickleberry for the murder. He also has some further claims that Carl Dunston was responsible for the death of Jack Warden.

"Jack Warden?" The sheriff said. He was killed by a grizzly. How can Dunston be responsible for that.

"I may be able to help you with that." I inserted.

"Enlighten me." The sheriff stated.

"Leif Peterson worked for Dunston and was a bear trapper. He trapped the grizzly and set up Jack Warden, surprised him on the trail, and released the grizzly on him. I know Peterson worked for Dunston and Dunston benefited from the death of Jack Warden. He also profited from the death of Leif Peterson and the execution of Mickleberry for the murder of Peterson. The only person that benefitted from all of these deaths was Carl Dunston."

The sheriff shook his head saying.

"You claim that you were kidnapped by a man working
for Dunston and held in a cabin. You have a note that says 'Close your store or Chauncey dies' is this correct?"

"It is."

"And why do you think Carl Dunston is responsible for this? Who was the man that kidnapped you?"

"He didn't tell me his name. He did tell me that Carl hired him to intimidate the store owners into shutting down so his stores would benefit. He also told me that he thought Mike Tompkins was the one that killed Leif Peterson, not the man named Mickleberry. He was going up to Coeur D'Alene to find Tompkins. He was scared of what would Carl would do to him and thought that if the real murderer of Peterson was revealed he would be safe."

"This is a lot to take in." The sheriff said. "I'm going to talk to Dunston and see what he has to say."

Chapter 45   The Trial

The Sheriff went to the home of Carl Dunston later that day. He knocked on the door. Nobody answered. He knocked again. He saw Nancy Dunston approaching the door. She opened it and the Sheriff noticed that her eyes were red and swollen.

"Is this a bad time?" He asked.

"I don't know if it will ever be any better." She quipped.

"I suppose you are here about the murders?"

"Well, I uh wanted to talk to Carl about some things." The Sheriff stuttered.

"He isn't here. Don't know where he went, and quite frankly, Sheriff, I don't care."

"I've had some men that came into my —" She stopped him mid sentence.

"I heard from Barton the telegraph man. He is claiming that Carl had Jack killed and that he also had Leif and others killed. How would you feel if you found out you married a man that killed your husband and other men as well? When I questioned Carl about it this afternoon he laughed at me and said that it was all foolishness. Then he left."

"Nancy, I need to ask you if Carl ever told you anything that indicated he had certain people eliminated."

"You mean like my former husband?" She said mockingly.

"I understand how hard this is for you, but I am a friend of Carl's also and if you know something, I need to hear it."

"OK, Sheriff. About six months ago, Carl had been drinking most of the evening and was in a rather happy mood. He said 'Leif has outlived his usefulness and I don't need him taking my hard earned money when he really isn't earning it'. I ask him what he was talking about. He said 'Leif and I have a deal for Leif to be my protector, what do I need protection from now? I have everything I want and nobody to challenge me'. This was right after Mickleberry had threatened Leif and Carl in a drunken stupor. Three days later, Leif was dead and Mickleberry was in jail."

"Do you have reason to believe that Carl had something to do with Leif's death?" The Sheriff queried.

"I do." Nancy replied. "The evening Carl heard that Leif was dead, he took me out to a special dinner 'celebration' he called it. He told me our profits have just increased by forty percent. What do you think Sheriff? I found out long ago that Carl doesn't have a sympathetic bone in his body."

"OK. I guess you have answered my questions about Carl. I am sorry to have bothered you, Mrs. Dunston." The Sheriff said as he left.

When the Sheriff got back to his office there was a Deputy there that told him he had received a report of a crazy man up at the Nine-Mile Cemetery. He's shooting a gun and talking crazy.

"Let's head up there." The Sheriff said.
When they arrived at the cemetery Carl Dunston could be heard yelling and cursing, shooting every which direction.

"I killed you all once." He yelled. "I can kill you again." He shot at a gravestone.

"I am going to be the Governor of Idaho and you need

to leave me alone." He said as he shot again.
The Sheriff called to him.

"Carl, it's me, your friend. Put your pistol down and let's talk."
Carl looked at him and said.

"Oh hi, Mel, how you been?"
The Sheriff and Deputy took Carl to the jail and locked him up.

The trial of Carl Dunston one month after his arrest was a big event. The courtroom was packed. People crowded around outside to hear any tidbit they could about the proceedings. Witnesses were called to testify: Buster Lucas, Chauncey and Franklin Miller, Mike Tompkins, and even Nancy Warden Dunston. Nancy Dunston obtained a divorce from Carl Dunston one week after he was arrested. She had her legal name changed back to Nancy Warden.

Several miners testified that Carl had one of their friends killed who had been involved with organizing a union in the Sierra Mine owned by Carl. The judge listened intently to other citizens that came forward to testify about how Carl was talking to himself on the streets of Wallace, and how he was talking about running for Governor of Idaho even though there was no election for two years. The Sheriff testified about the crazy scene at the Nine-Mile Cemetery where Carl was talking to gravestones, shooting at phantoms. Franklin Miller testified that Carl, then known as Bart Decker, had killed their father in Goshen, Indiana. Chauncey Miller testified that he had been kidnapped by a man that wanted his family to shut down their store that was competing with Carl's store. Chauncey produced a note that said "Shut down your store, or Chauncey dies".

The defense attorney had little in defense of Carl other than what he had done for the community of Wallace. He also claimed hat no one had ever seen or could prove Carl killed a single person. He called Carl to the witness stand and asked him if he killed Leif Peterson and Jack Warden or any other men. Carl said.

"No, of course not, I just talked to them yesterday. How could I kill them? They are not dead."
When Carl returned to his seat he continued talking and gesturing to nobody in particular.

In the end, all of the remaining witnesses were very credible explaining a multitude of Carl's faults and transgressions. When the final testimony had been heard, the judge said he would pronounce the verdict the following day, but before his decision he wanted to talk to Carl in the presence of only his defense attorney and the prosecutor.

The three men went into the Judge's chambers. He asked them all to sit down. He then asked Carl a series of questions.

"Carl, I want you to tell me what date it is today."
Carl looked puzzled.

"It is the 4th of July." He answered. "Fireworks tonight."

"Carl, can you tell me what city you are in right now?"
This time Carl didn't hesitate. "Virginia City."

"Carl, what state were you born in?"

"Montana."

"Carl how old are you?"
The prosecutor interrupted.

"Judge, you must be kidding. This man is not that confused. He is just faking stupidity, or whatever he is trying to do, to make you believe he is incompetent."

The Judge replied.

"Excuse me, Mr. Prosecutor, I am doing the questioning here, and I will be the judge of whether he is competent or not. The defense attorney did not say a word. The Judge continued his questions.

"Carl, how old are you?"

"Eighteen."

"What year were you born?" The judge quickly asked.

"1852." He replied.

"Carl, that would make you almost fifty years old."

"I'M EIGHTEEN YEARS OLD." Carl screamed.

"Carl, what was the name of the mine that you owned?"

"What mine?" Carl said.

"Was it the Silver Slipper?" The Judge asked.

"Yeah, that was it." Carl responded. "The Silver Sleeper. I did own that mine, didn't I?

"What happened to that mine, Carl?

"I sold it last week."

"What year is it?" The Judge quickly asked.

"1870." Carl answered just as quickly.

The Judge said.

"I have heard enough. I will give you my decision tomorrow."

The Defense attorney and the Prosecutor both yelped.

"Don't we get to ask him anything?"

"NO! You are dismissed. You will have my decision tomorrow."

The following day the judge proclaimed Carl Dunston to be incompetent and unable to understand the charges against him by reason of insanity. He committed Carl Dunston to a hospital for the criminally insane in Blackfoot, Idaho.

As Carl was escorted from the courtroom, Bull Lukas was

seated in the back row by the doorway. Carl walked by and slowed down as he approached Bull. He winked at Bull as he passed him and went through the doorway smiling a smug smile.

Chapter 46   Wedding

Gabrielle and I decided that it was time to set a date for our wedding. David was anxious for us to get married also. Gabrielle told me that before I got kidnapped again or I got eaten by a grizzly again; we really needed to set that date. We set the following month on July 9th as our wedding day.

We were married in the Methodist Church in Wallace on July 9th. Franklin was my best man and David was a groomsman. Maureen was the Maid of Honor and Charlene Lucas was a bridesmaid. David and Charlene were both twelve years old and made a nice couple as they walked down the aisle. Gabrielle wore a dress that Abigail made just for her, and it was a very beautiful dress for a very beautiful lady. As Gabrielle walked down the aisle toward me, I reflected on how lucky I was to be here. I had come from Indiana to Idaho, survived a bear attack and a kidnapping. I was indeed lucky to have found Gabrielle and lucky to be alive to marry her.

After the wedding we went to the Silverback Steakhouse that had been closed for our reception dinner. Maureen and her mother set up a buffet that was fit for a king and queen. They served elk and beef steaks, fresh cantaloupe, raspberries, blueberries, huckleberries, green beans, squash, and carrots, buttered new potatoes, and a large three tiered wedding cake with a miniature couple on top and a little grizzly bear behind them. After the reception, there was a shiny new Model T Ford car out in front of the restaurant that my brother Franklin had bought us for a wedding present. Gabrielle and I would learn to drive a car on our honeymoon.

David was excited to stay with the Lukas family while we went on our honeymoon. He and Charlene had become good friends and both of them were looking forward to us leaving them. Gabrielle told Abigail that she should keep a close eye on those two.

On our honeymoon we drove all the way to the Yellowstone National Park in Wyoming and stayed at the Mammoth Hot Springs Inn for three nights and the Old Faithful Inn for three nights. During the days we traveled to all of the sights, sounds, and smells of the famous park. We saw spewing geysers, mud pots, bubbling fumaroles, giant waterfalls, beautiful snow capped mountains, steaming ponds, and lots of buffalo, moose and elk (no grizzlies). We both agreed that travelling by car was far superior to riding on horseback. We saw such beautiful scenery while driving the road down to Wyoming. The road from Missoula to Bozeman was actually paved with something called asphalt. It was a great improvement from the rutted dusty road that we had driven from Wallace to Missoula.

When we returned to Wallace, Gabrielle and I moved into the new house we had purchased in Wallace prior to the wedding. It would be our winter home and the cabin on the North Fork would be out summer ranch home. I had cashed in more gold before the wedding, and had a large bankroll which was used to purchase the home and some furniture. David, Gabrielle and I were now a family. Gabrielle and

David worked at Gabbi and Abbi's Store during the week. Franklin and I resumed his building business like we had in Missoula. There was less demand for housing than in Missoula but we still had enough work to keep us comfortably busy.

I officially adopted David as my son in late summer. I now had a teenager, since David turned thirteen years old in August. He was attending school and had found many friends in Wallace in addition to his best friend, Charlene Lukas. David, Gabrielle and I still had time to go hunting occasionally. Gabrielle, however, was so busy with the store that she didn't have a lot of spare time. In December, I found out from Gabrielle that we were going to have a baby. I was thrilled, even though I would be rather old by the time the child was a teenager. That did not diminish my enthusiasm.

In August Gabby gave birth to a six pound six ounce, bouncing baby girl that we named Jessica Rose Miller. The entire gang of Franklin, Maureen and their son Jacob, Bull, Abigail and Charlene Lukas (their two boys had joined the army) and Maureen's mother Patricia, were on hand for the birth. Patricia had been a midwife prior to becoming a chef and was able assist Gabby with the birth. Morgan was very interested in the new member of the family and would lie down next to her crib when she was sleeping. He even would come and get us when she awoke.

Rumors had spread quickly around Wallace that Carl Dunston had escaped from the asylum in Blackfoot. Blackfoot was near Pocatello Idaho which was over three hundred miles away from Wallace. I had resigned myself to the fact that Bart Decker or Carl Dunston was no longer a concern of mine. As Chief Big Foot and Screaming Eagle had told us, there is no positive benefit from seeking revenge. If my center of attention was concentrated on Bart Decker and his activities, I would lose focus on my own life.

Since leaving my home in Indiana I have gained so much insight into what I was really seeking in life. I was looking to find a meaning why our father had been taken from us and why I had emptiness in my soul. I have found the answers to both of those questions. I have the meaning in my life that I had always sought. It was all around me. My family, my home, my Idaho. They were the things that meant the most to me now. Bart Decker was a bad dream from which I had awakened. He no longer was meaningful to me.

Chapter 47   Revenge

Nancy Dunston Warden, however, had not gotten over Carl Dunston. Back when she had suspicions of Carl not being honest with her she searched for reasons to dispel those fears. When Carl was out of town she searched his office. In the office she found substance to her suspicions and her fears took on a new life. Carl had papers that showed he was sending money to a bank in Ogden, Utah. Lots of money. The papers Nancy found showed the transfer of over one-hundred thousand dollars from his accounts in Wallace to the bank in Ogden. Nancy was an astute business woman. While Carl was busy fighting the union at his Sierra Mine, Nancy told him she was going to visit her sister in Portland. Instead she took a different trip down to Ogden, Utah.

Along with her, She took her marriage license and some other documents. She went to the Bank of Ogden and introduced herself as Carl Dunston's wife Nancy Dunston, showing the bank manager her identification. She explained that Carl had sent her to make some changes to their account.

"He wishes me to make some transfers of our money. He is concerned that he should not have so much money invested in one bank. We want to transfer seventy five thousand dollars of the money to two different banks; one bank in Logan, Utah and one in Brigham City in joint accounts."

The banker was reluctant to make the changes.

"You are not a cosigner on the account." He stated.

"The truth of the matter is." Nancy said. "Carl is not well, and cannot travel. He has given this letter for me to show you in case you did not agree to the transfers."

She showed the bank manager a letter of introduction requesting that his wishes be carried out to the fullest. It was signed by Carl Dunston and notarized by an official at the Bank of Wallace.

The banker compared the signatures on the account with the signature on the letter.

"Well, this changes everything." The banker said. "We will be glad to make your changes."

"Carl also told me if there was any problem, that I should remove all of our money from your bank."

"I am sorry you feel that way. I'm sure we can work something out." He said.

"He was very clear on that." Nancy replied. "Please transfer half of the money to the Logan Bank, and the other half to the Brigham City Bank."

"As you wish." The manger replied.

After leaving Ogden, Nancy went to the Brigham City bank the following day and withdrew the entire amount in a cashier's check. She did the same at the Logan Bank. On her way home she stopped at a bank in Pocatello Idaho and made a deposit of over one-hundred thousand dollars in the name of Nancy Warden. She told the bank that this was a private account and that no information about her account should be revealed to any person inquiring or she would remove the money. One hundred thousand dollars was a lot of money even to a bank. The banker told Nancy that her account would be marked confidential so that she was the only person with access. When Carl Dunston was arrested and jailed for the murders of her husband, Leif Peterson and others, Nancy was thankful that she had transferred the funds into another bank in her name.

When Nancy heard about Carl's escape from the Mental Hospital in Blackfoot, she wondered how long it would take for him to discover his missing funds in Ogden. She decided that she would be proactive. She traveled down to Ogden, Utah. She rented a room at a hotel across the street from the Bank of Ogden.

She watched from her hotel window day after day. She began to think she must have missed Carl. She wasn't sure how much more time she could sit staring out a window. On the fourth day of observing, she saw him coming down the street. He was disheveled and had a long scruffy beard. His face was gaunt and he was much thinner than he had ever been. He did have a suit on but it did not fit him well and he appeared nervous as he kept looking around uneasily. Nancy almost felt sorry for the pathetic man that she saw. Almost, but no, because she remembered what he did to Jack and to her. Carl Dunston walked into the bank as Nancy watched intently from the hotel.

She waited for almost fifteen minutes. All of the sudden Carl came bursting out of the bank doors in a fury. He was turning back to the bank and yelling. She could hear him even from across the street.

"I am going to sue you. You can't do this. I did not authorize that." He was waving his arms and gesturing wildly.

Nancy smiled. "Serves you right." She muttered to herself. But she was not done with Carl. She watched Carl go into a hotel a block down the street. Nancy put on the blonde wig and fancy hat she had purchased and a pair of sunglasses. She walked down to the hotel and sat down in the lobby. She waited.

That evening Carl walked through the lobby and went down the street to a saloon. He stayed in the saloon for several hours. Nancy waited in an alleyway outside of the saloon. It was dark and raining lightly for the past hour. Nancy was drenched and cold, but resolute. She kept thinking of her husband Jack being mauled and killed by a grizzly bear. That kept her firm on her mission. She would wait until snow flew if she had to. She could not believe that she had been duped by this shyster.

Carl finally came stumbling out of the saloon at midnight and headed directly toward her. Nancy spoke as Carl walked past.

"Hey, honey. You want some action?"
Carl in his stupor was interested by the female voice, but did not recognize Nancy in the dark. She motioned for him to follow her. He followed. When they reached the back of the alley, Nancy turned.

"Hi, Carl." She said. "I have a message from Jack. You aren't the only one that has been talking to him."
Carl realized who was talking to him at the same time he saw the pearl handled pistol that was pointing directly at him.

"Nancy, Honey. I, I have been — "
"Save your lies, Carl. I don't want to hear them. Or should I say Bart."

Carl's eyes were wild, like a trapped animal, traveling rapidly back and forth as he searched for an escape from this dilemma. Nancy saw the eyes darting.

"Too late for a way out, Carl. You sealed your fate when you had my husband killed. A grizzly bear, Carl? How could you. At least Jack had some integrity, something you have never had."

"But Nan---" A shot rang out. Carl looked at Nancy in disbelief. Then he looked down at the growing red stain on his stomach.

"I loved you, Nancy, I really did."

Another shot reverberated in the alley and Carl slumped to the ground.

"Liar!" Was all that Nancy said as she turned and strode away.

Chapter 48   Bart is Dead

The word had gotten to Wallace that Carl Dunston had been found in Ogden, Utah. He had been found shot in an alley. He was not dead, but in bad shape. When the Sheriff in Ogden questioned him about who had shot him, he said he did not know who it was. It all happened too fast he told them. They took my money, was all he said. Carl Dunston died, two days after he had been shot. He died alone with no one coming to visit. The shooter was never identified.

A funeral was held in Wallace two days after Carl's death, since Wallace had been his home. The service was held in the local funeral parlor. Three people showed up for the funeral. Chauncey Miller, Franklin Miller and Buster Bull Lukas. It was a short and sad service. Carl, formerly the richest man in Wallace, was given a pauper's ceremony. He was buried at the Nine Mile Cemetery.

I had a strange sensation attending the funeral. This was the man I had searched so long and so hard to find. I had anticipated that I would have a sense of relief being there at the funeral of Bart Decker. I had no such sense of relief. I felt sadness. Bart Decker came from a home where there was no love and no relationship with his family.

Bull told me about all of the beatings and trauma that Bart had endured as a child. Bart had sought something to make him feel whole. Bull could not supply that. Money did not provide that. Nancy Dunston was unable to supply it. Bart was a broken man, and nothing could repair the damage that had been done to him as a small boy. Bart Decker never found happiness. It appears that his life had been taken from him by a common thief. This may have been what he deserved, but I wasn't convinced of that. My dealings with Bart had been limited; but he certainly must have had some redeeming qualities.

Franklin, Bull and I rode up to the Nine Mile Cemetery for the interment. We watched as the casket was lowered into the ground. The cemetery workers began shoveling the dirt into the grave. Bull said:

"Farewell, old friend. I am sorry things turned out so bad for you."

A simple marker was put on the grave that would forever be the sum total of Carl Dunston's life. It said:

"Carl Dunston 1908 RIP".

Chapter 49   Chauncey is Happy

Five years have passed and many things have changed in Wallace. Automobiles are now everywhere in town. People have electricity and there are street lights in town. Still no electricity at my cabin though. Our store had to be expanded with the demand for more goods. Jessica is now four years of age and talking a blue streak. Franklin and Maureen's son, Jacob, is six and he and Jessica have fun playing together. They also have another playmate, Annette, who is the one year old daughter of Maureen and Franklin.

David is eighteen years old now and has just signed up to join the Army . He wants to join the Air Corp flying planes. There are rumors of war in Europe. Gabrielle and I are concerned about the possibility of David being sent overseas. Franklin and I built very nice houses side by side up on a hill overlooking the town. We have nice views of the whole city and winding river below us.

Gabrielle, David and I have gone to our cabin on the North Fork of the Coeur D'Alene every summer. We fish, hunt and occasionally trap bear. I always make the bear traps small since I did not want to deal with another large silverback. We own several properties in Wallace that we rent out to families. I also purchased interest in a silver mine located on Nine Mile Road less than a mile from downtown. We are making a nice profit from the mine.

The Silverback Steak House is the premier restaurant in Wallace. It rivals the success of the Hellgate Steakhouse in Missoula. I was pleased with what our families have done in the city. The Miller families are well known and respected. It makes us proud. Our trip from Indiana out west was the best decision that Franklin and I have ever made. I also think how traveling to Prichard to buy a pick axe and ended up meeting David, Gabrielle and Morgan was fortuitous. Maureen and her mother just happened to find Abigail Lukas who led us to locating Bull. Abigail, when she came to Wallace to visit, recognized Bart Decker in the General Store. Life is full of happenstance. Existence would be dull were it not for the unexpected.

I look forward to the future. My little daughter asks:
"Daddy, when can I go hunt grizzly bears with you?"
"Soon." I tell her. But I am not anxious for her to grow up too fast. It already seems like yesterday that I held her in my arms for the first time. Time is an endless army marching to battle. We will never win the battle with time. It can never be recovered, only remembered. So I cherish the memories and look forward to the next battle with time that is just around the corner of my mind.

Epilogue

C hauncey Miller was my father's uncle who trapped
bear and mined silver in Northern Idaho. He homesteaded a
thirty acre parcel of land on the North Fork of the Coeur
D'Alene River ten miles north of the town called Prichard.
My father, Carter Logan, traveled to Idaho when he was only
twenty years old to spend the summer with his Uncle
Chauncey in the year 1920. He travelled alone by train to
Missoula, Montana and had to take a bus to Prichard. The
only directions that he had were: follow the North Fork of the
Coeur D'Alene River ten miles upstream and the cabin will be
on the north side of the river. I asked him if he was afraid. He
told me that he ran the entire ten miles up to the cabin.

While there, Chauncey showed my father how he trapped
bear and lived off of the land. One of my early memories as a
child was a bear skin rug that hung on the wall of our garage.
It was a bear that my father and Chauncey had trapped in
Idaho. My mother refused to allow the moth-eaten thing (as
she referred to it) in the house. My father told me stories about
Idaho and of one incident when a "large bear" tore apart one
of their traps.

Chauncey's sister Annette (or Nettie as she was called) was
my Grandmother. I chose to write a fictional story about why
her brother, Chauncey, traveled out West ending up in Idaho.
I was never able to learn the real reasons that he undertook

this journey to a very wild and unknown part of the country.

Chauncey's father did actually die before he was born, but I was unable to find information about how he died in 1864. Possibly he died in the Civil War, but that too is speculation.

Chauncey Miller died of unknown cause in 1930 in Wallace, Idaho and is buried at the Nine-Mile Cemetery north of Wallace. I found his gravestone at that cemetery on a site called "findagrave.com".

My mind's eye led me to the scenario that I chose to explain Jacob Miller's death and the eventual decision of Chauncey and his brother, Franklin, to travel out West ending up in Northern Idaho. I attempted to put a historical flavor to the experiences of Chauncey and Franklin while traveling from Goshen, Indiana to Missoula, Montana, and then eventually to Idaho. Much of what transpired in the book is based upon actual historical happenings during that time period.

In researching my Great Uncle I requested information from the Shoshone County Recorder's office in Wallace, Idaho. I discovered that Chauncey owned five properties in the Wallace area including a silver mine and several houses in addition to the 30 acre property that he had homesteaded on the North Fork. I assume that due to the dire conditions of this time due to the Great Depression; that none of his family were able to travel to Idaho to lay claim to his properties.

I was pleasantly surprised to find this article in the June 6, 1929 edition of the Spokane Daily Chronicle as follows:

TROUT STRIKING

*Trout fishing…reported excellent near Chauncey Miller's
ranch on the upper North Fork of the Coeur d"Alene river, a
favorite spot, for fisherman of the Coeur d'Alenes, According
to Mr. Miller who returned yesterday to Wallace, Idaho, from
a two week outing at the ranch. He brought in a limit catch,
some trout weighing three pounds.*

From this article I ascertained that Chauncey, in his later
years, would live in the city of Wallace during the winter and
use his cabin as a summer "ranch" as he called it.

Chauncey never married, but that didn't fit the story I had
in my mind: so I changed it. It could have happened. I would
really like to have learned the reasons for Chauncey going to
Idaho; but there is no family available that knew why, and my
father never found out or never asked.

Parents: explain things to your children about your family
history, or some future writer in your family could make up
tales about them that may be a total work of fiction. If you are
related to the Jacob and Mary Ann Stutzman Miller families
from the Goshen, Indiana area; I would love to hear from you.
You can contact me at gdlogan44@yahoo.com.

Gary D Logan

Pictures

These are some actual pictures near Chauncey's property in his later years. Please remember that these pictures are almost one hundred years old and as such have survived quite well.

North Fork of Coeur D'Alene River near Cabin
Around 1920

Another North Fork picture near the Cabin

The Cabin as it was in 1920. Fenced area is part of the garden.

Chauncey's garden. Looks like Idaho potatoes.

Winter in Northern Idaho

My Dad, Carter Logan, at the Little Guard Lookout in 1920 when he visited Chauncey. This is three and one-half miles north of the cabin.

Chauncey cutting lumber. The burned hill in the background was from a major fire called the "Big Blow" that swept through the entire Northwest in 1910.

Chauncey in his garden with Morgan. He was in his sixties when this was taken. Notice the shallow pan in the foreground. He really did pan for gold.

North Fork across from Chauncey's cabin